Alice Dodd
and the
Spirit of Truth

Alice Dodd
and the
Spirit of Truth

by Catherine Frey Murphy

MACMILLAN PUBLISHING COMPANY   NEW YORK

MAXWELL MACMILLAN CANADA   TORONTO

MAXWELL MACMILLAN INTERNATIONAL
NEW YORK   OXFORD   SINGAPORE   SYDNEY

Macmillan Publishing Company is part of the Maxwell Communication Group of Companies. Macmillan Publishing Company, 866 Third Avenue, New York, NY 10022. Maxwell Macmillan Canada, Inc., 1200 Eglinton Avenue East, Suite 200, Don Mills, Ontario M3C 3N1.

First edition
Printed in the United States of America

1   3   5   7   9   10   8   6   4   2

The text of this book is set in 11 point Bembo.

Library of Congress Cataloging-in-Publication Data
Murphy, Catherine Frey.
   Alice Dodd and the spirit of truth / by Catherine Frey Murphy.—1st ed.
     p.   cm.
   Summary: While spending the summer in a vacation cabin with her aunt and three-year-old cousin, a young girl finds herself more and more involved in a series of lies and deceptions.
   ISBN 0-02-767702-8
   [1. Honesty—Fiction.   2. Interpersonal relations—Fiction.
3. Self-acceptance—Fiction.   4. Vacations—Fiction.]   I. Title.
PZ7.M9523A1   1993   [Fic]—dc20   92-32039

For my grandfather, Dr. Edwin Hardy Ober

1

I began my first summer away from my parents by lying to my Aunt Kate. I didn't exactly mean to. I had planned to stick to the truth, but things seemed to get out of hand right from the start.

I woke up early that first morning in my family's summer cabin, my favorite place in the world. No sound came from the other bedroom, where Aunt Kate and my three-year-old cousin, Amy, were sleeping; except for the racket of birds outside, the cabin was quiet.

Sunlight sifted through the leaves of the beech tree outside the window and picked out the place on the wall of my room where the names of everyone in our family were marked next to our heights. Every summer we measured everybody, even the grown-ups, and marked the measurements on that wall. Every year my grandpa's line got a little higher than the year before. He insisted that he was still growing, but I thought he stood on his tiptoes.

My name was on that wall eleven times, once for every year of my life except this one. The wall was a smeared clutter of names, from baby measurements down near the floor to the highest marks of all, close to the ceiling, for my dad and my basketball-playing brother, Joe. Some of the names were so faded they were hard to read. Those were for my mother and Aunt Kate when they were little girls, with the dates of summers they used to spend here long before I was born.

I hopped out of bed, stood against the wall, and flattened my hand on top of my head. Then I twisted out from under my hand to search through the pencil marks for the one that showed how tall I had been the year before. I found the mark—not very high up; I'm short, like my mother—and frowned at my name, written in my mother's neat block letters: "Alice Dodd."

What an ugly name, I thought, so plain and dull. No magic at all. I grabbed a pencil and drew a line at my new height, pressing hard so that the marks would stand out. "Alexis Deveraux," I wrote, and stood back to study the effect. It looked a lot better.

A small voice began to sing, entirely off-key, in the other bedroom. From what I could hear through the wall, the words of the song were, "I am awake, where is my cereal? I am awake, where is my cereal?"

I dropped the pencil and reached for my clothes. My summer job—taking care of Amy so that Aunt Kate could paint—was about to start.

Aunt Kate and Amy's father, my Uncle Tony, got divorced when Amy was a baby. After that Aunt Kate didn't have much money. She designed cornflake boxes and soup ads in New York City to make a living. But this summer she had sublet her apartment and she was staying at the cabin, where she didn't have to pay rent, so that she could paint what she wanted to. I had arrived the night before, and I was supposed to start watching Amy this morning.

I'd never spent much time alone with Amy, and I wasn't sure what to expect. From the singing and yelling I could hear coming from the other room, it sounded as if she might keep me pretty busy.

Whatever taking care of Amy was like, it couldn't be much worse than staying home in Massachusetts for the summer. My mother had decided to teach summer school this year, so she and my father were both at work all day. And my friends were all off someplace, at camp, or on vacations, or visiting their fathers in other states because their parents were divorced. Even Chloe, my best and oldest friend ever since nursery school, had gone off to computer camp in Vermont for the whole summer, leaving me all by myself.

When I was younger, that would have been okay. I would have just tagged along with my older brother, Joe, all summer. But not this year. At the thought of Joe, I stopped buttoning my shorts and scowled at his name on the wall so far above my head.

Joe was four years older than I, and he had always been smarter, faster, bigger, and better in every way—or so it seemed to me. He was a star basketball player, and at the top of his class, and president of student government, and besides all that, he was the good-looking one in the family. At the beginning of every school year my teachers would say, "Oh, you're Joe Dodd's sister!" They seemed to expect me to be wonderful, just like him. But every year they were disappointed, because I never turned out to be quite as good at things as he was.

Oh, I was smart enough—my grades were okay. Not at the top of the class, but not at the bottom, either. And I did pretty well in sports and band and things like that, though I wasn't a star. I was always in the middle, that was the trouble. I didn't stand out at anything. I seemed to be—well, very medium.

I didn't mind when I was younger—I just followed Joe around, and did whatever he told me to, and generally adored him. Joe was my best buddy, even if he was a superstar, and we used to have a lot of fun.

But last year I had started to resent always being in his shadow. I got tired of always seeing his name in the paper for honor roll or for some basketball trophy. And I was tired, too, of having my friends ask where my cute brother Joe was as soon as they stepped into my house, as if they were there to see him instead of me. I wished I could be more like Joe. But how? Everything I could think of to do, Joe already did better. It was hopeless. I would never catch up with him.

I sighed and decided not to think about Joe anymore. This was my summer away, after all—my first real chance to get off on my own. I had jumped at the opportunity when Aunt Kate called to ask if I could come to the cabin for the summer to take care of Amy.

I could still hear Amy singing in the other bedroom, and from the sound of it, jumping on the bed. "Hey," came Aunt Kate's sleepy voice. "Amy, don't bounce on me!"

I pulled my T-shirt over my head, ran my fingers through my short hair, and headed for the kitchen, tripping over the duffel bag I'd left on the floor the night before. Grandpa had picked me up at the bus station in Binghamton, where he lives. It had been late when we arrived at the cabin, in the hills outside the city, and Amy was already in bed. I had been so sleepy that I had barely managed to say hello to Aunt Kate before I staggered into the little bedroom that was mine every summer and fell asleep on top of the covers. Grandpa must have gone home sometime after that, but I hadn't heard him leave.

Now the kitchen was full of yellow light, and the familiar green linoleum was cool under my bare toes. A thud from the bedroom shook the floor, and Amy, in a flowered nightgown, galloped in. "Boom!" she yelled, hopping around the kitchen, her dark, tangled curls bouncing on her shoulders. "Hi, Alice! I jumped off the bed! I'm a jumping horsie! I want some breakfast!"

I hadn't realized that such a little girl could make so much noise. "Okay," I said doubtfully, and opened a cabinet. "Let's see. Do jumping horsies like Cheerios?"

"Yes!" shouted Amy, just as loudly as before. "My bunny wants some, too!" She climbed onto the bench by the pine table and carefully propped a grubby pink bunny next to her. Aunt Kate's voice came from the bedroom, not so sleepy now.

"Thanks for feeding her, Alice," she called. "I'll be out in a minute."

Amy kept singing at the top of her lungs while I poured out the Cheerios, but she quieted down, finally, when she began to eat. My ears were still ringing when I sat down across from her with my own bowl of Cheerios, while Amy took turns feeding dribbling spoonfuls of cereal to herself and to her stuffed bunny.

It was after Aunt Kate came out of the bedroom that I told the lie. Maybe it was because of the way she looked. Aunt Kate didn't look like an aunt, or like anybody's mother. Even in an old T-shirt and ragged, paint-stained jeans, she looked like a princess. She had high cheekbones spattered with freckles, and large eyes, bright blue like

Grandpa's, that seemed to have a light of their own. She had never cut her wavy black hair short, the way most mothers did, and it rippled past her waist, like Rapunzel's.

"Amy, be careful, please! You're getting Cheerios all over everything." Aunt Kate sounded more like my mother on a grouchy morning than like a fairy-tale princess.

"Okay, Mommy," Amy said sweetly, and fed another dripping spoonful to her bunny.

Aunt Kate sighed as she ran water into the teakettle and set it on the stove. "Oh, I give up," she said with a tired smile. "At least she's having fun. Good morning, Alice."

"Hi, Aunt Kate," I said. In my T-shirt and cutoffs, I felt about as interesting as my chair. It was hard for me to believe I was related to my Aunt Kate. She was my mother's sister, but they didn't look alike. I looked like my mother, who was little and plump, with glasses and dull, feathery brown hair. Lately, I had been trying not to look so much like my mother. But the more I did things to my hair, and picked out unusual clothes, and practiced holding my face in different expressions, the more people stopped me in the post office to say, "Alice Anne Dodd, you are the very image of your mother!"

"So tell me, Alice." Aunt Kate's hair swung around her like a cloak as she turned toward me. "You fell asleep so fast last night that we didn't get a chance to talk. What's your life like, now that you're twelve and almost grown up?"

"My life?" I floundered, surprised. "Well, there's school, of course. And—um—my friends and I do stuff together. And I do housework for Mom since she went back to work. And—well, I read a lot. That's about it, I guess."

Aunt Kate raised an eyebrow. "That bad, huh? Come on, Alice, you're exaggerating."

"Nope," I said glumly. "I never exaggerate. I have the dullest life on the planet Earth."

"Hmm." Aunt Kate seemed to be hiding a smile. "Well, tell me about the dullest life on the planet Earth, then. What's your ruling passion?"

"My what?" I asked, feeling stupid.

"You know, your ruling passion. Something you like best to do, or to think about. Something you care about. Something you're good at." Aunt Kate smiled at me encouragingly.

I stared at her blankly. Good at? I didn't seem to be particularly good at anything; that was the whole trouble with my life. I seemed to be a lot like my boring, ordinary name—just plain dull.

But I didn't want my beautiful, talented aunt to think that I was dull, even if that was the truth. At least I could invent something interesting. So I opened my mouth and the lie popped out, and I think that was the moment when everything about that summer began to go wrong.

"Well," I said, "I've been getting interested in art and—um—doing some drawing. I did a drawing of an owl, and I put it in a contest at school, and I won!"

It was partly true, at least. I had tried to draw a barred owl that I had seen at a nature center where our class went on a field trip. I had stared at the owl for a long time. It had looked friendly, somehow, blinking and clicking its beak as if it were just about to tell me a great joke. When we got back to school, I had tried to draw it. I wanted to show the way everything about the owl was round and brown, the same curves over and over again, even in the comical look on its little round face.

But the drawing didn't look comical and friendly, or even like an owl at all. It looked stupid. I did enter it in the contest, because the teacher said we had to enter something. But it didn't win, and I knew that was because I didn't have any talent for art. As far as I could tell, I didn't have any talent for anything. But it seemed impossible, just then, to let Aunt Kate know that.

"That's terrific, Alice!" said Aunt Kate.

"Well, it won second prize," I amended guiltily, as if scaling down the lie would make it somehow not so bad.

"I'd like to see that drawing. Did you bring it with you?" she asked as she poured out a mugful of tea.

"Um, no. It's at home," I said uncomfortably. Already I wished I could unsay what I'd said. But then Amy stuck her elbow into her cereal bowl, spilling milk and Cheerios all over herself and the table. Aunt Kate grabbed a sponge and I jumped up to help, and we were both so busy for a minute or two that she stopped asking me awkward questions.

By the time the table and Amy were cleaned up and Amy had gone off to the toy box in the corner to play, Aunt Kate seemed to have forgotten all about my imaginary art award. At least, I hoped she had. She sat down across from me with her tea.

"Whew," she said. "Sometimes Amy wears me out. I hope she won't be too much for you, Alice."

"Oh, no," I said, more confidently than I really felt, but relieved that we had gotten off the subject of the art contest.

"I've done a lot of baby-sitting." This was true. I had watched my neighbors' toddler a number of times while his mother ran to the grocery store. I didn't mention to Aunt Kate that I had only done this during nap times, while he was sound alseep, and that his mother had always gotten back before he woke up.

"Are you too tired to watch her for an hour or two this morning?"

"No, no, I'm fine." I tried not to glance anxiously at Amy, who had already hauled all the toys out of the toy box and was now sitting in the middle of the mess, trying to pull the head off one of my old dolls.

"Well, good," said Aunt Kate. She smiled at me through the steam rising from her mug. "To tell the truth, I can hardly wait to get to work."

"What are you working on?" I asked curiously.

"Well, I guess you could call it an imaginary landscape. It's my idea of the kingdom of Atlantis."

"Atlantis? Where's that?"

"Nobody knows," said Aunt Kate. "It's a place the ancient Greeks told stories about, a mythical kingdom on an island that sank into the sea."

"Was it a real place?"

"Most people don't think so. But I like to think it might have been."

"What was Atlantis like?" I asked, intrigued.

"Well, that's a mystery," said Aunt Kate. "That's why I wanted to paint it, I guess. I'm not stuck with the real world; I can invent it the way I want it to be. The possibilities are unlimited."

Atlantis. I savored the unfamiliar word as I ate my cereal.

It sounded wonderful: a lost kingdom on an island in the sea. A magical place, a place where anything might happen. A place of unlimited possibilities.

Aunt Kate set her mug down with a bang, as if she'd decided something. "Alice, if you really do feel ready to take care of Amy this morning, there are a few things I'd better tell you about before you get started."

Amy played happily in the mess of toys while Aunt Kate showed me her clothes and her potty chair, told me about her favorite games, pointed out some snacks in the kitchen, and reminded me to watch her all the time and never, never to lose track of the pink bunny, because Amy couldn't get along without it.

"I'll be right here in the sun porch if you need me," she said finally. "But try not to interrupt me if you don't have to, okay?"

"Not unless burglars come, or the house burns down, or there's a hurricane or something," I promised.

"Well, you don't have to let things get *that* bad." Aunt Kate kissed Amy on top of the head. "See you at lunchtime, honey bunch," she said, and stepped out onto the sun porch, where she had set up her painting things.

But then she popped her head back around the door. "Alice, maybe later you could do some drawings for me. It sounds as if we've got another artist in the family, and I'd like to see your work." Before I could answer her, she disappeared again, closing the porch door firmly behind her.

Amy abruptly stopped singing, stuck her thumb in her mouth, and eyed the closed door unhappily. I wasn't feeling very happy myself. I wasn't really sure that I could handle Amy all alone. And I wished I hadn't made up that story about the art contest.

I wanted Aunt Kate to think I was special. But I had never meant to tell her a fib. It wasn't as if I had fibbed about anything important, I told myself. It wasn't even a lie, really. Just an exaggeration. No matter what I'd told Aunt Kate about never exaggerating, anybody with a life as dull as mine had to exaggerate a little now and then, just to get along.

2

It didn't take Amy long to forget about sucking her thumb and staring sadly at the door. After only a minute or two, she brightened up and started tearing around the living room, making noises like a jet plane.

"Vroom! Vroom!" she shouted, climbing up onto the couch to see through the window. "Outside! Let's go outside!"

It seemed like a good idea. Maybe she wouldn't seem so loud outdoors. So I got her to hold still long enough to dress her in the shorts and striped T-shirt Aunt Kate had laid out for her, and we went out of the dim cabin into the bright warmth of the morning.

The breeze carried the clean, summery scent of grass and pine trees. Amy let out a joyful yell and charged across the yard. I followed her, walking backward to look at the cabin, making sure, I guess, that nothing had changed in the year since I'd last been there.

The cabin stood all by itself at the end of a lonely dirt road on a hilltop at the edge of the woods. Down in the valley beyond it, I could see pastures, cornfields and more woods, but no houses. Grandpa had built the cabin years ago, and our family had always spent summer vacations there. It was nothing fancy, just a small cottage, dark brown with yellow trim. But it looked beautiful to me.

Everything looked the way it always had: the beech tree,

the sagging old glider swing in the yard, the yellow window boxes with the geraniums that Grandma used to plant every year and Grandpa had planted since Grandma died a few years ago. The best thing about the cabin, I thought, was the way nothing there ever changed. I let out a sigh of satisfaction and turned back around.

Amy was at the other end of the yard already, and I had to run to catch up with her. "Hey, wait for me," I called. She was trotting along the dirt road that began at the cabin and led eventually down the hill to the village of Muskrat Falls in the valley. When I caught up with Amy, I suggested, "Let's go see the blackbird pond."

"Okay," she said cheerfully, and scampered ahead of me up the road. Not far off was an abandoned farm, the only other house on the hill. It had been empty for as long as I could remember, the house getting shabbier each year, the big old barn slowly falling down. There was a pond on the farm where red-winged blackbirds built their nests. Joe and I used to spend whole days there, fishing, wading, and holding swimming races that Joe always won—except when he let me win on purpose, and that was worse.

The only problem with the blackbird pond was that to get there you had to pass the witch house. That's what Joe had always called the abandoned farmhouse. It was rickety and unpainted, with loose shutters that banged in the wind and cracked, empty windows like crazy eyes. Joe and I used to grab each other's hands and run past it with our eyes squeezed shut. Joe dared me to go up onto the porch once, but I wouldn't do it. He teased me about it, but I noticed he didn't go up there, either.

As we got closer to the grove of pine trees just before the house, I took Amy's hand, still a little sticky from breakfast. It was ridiculous, I told myself, that after all these years I still felt nervous about a plain old empty house. Amy was singing loudly as we passed the pine trees and the house came into view. Her singing sounded just as loud outside as it had in the cabin, but just then, I thought her cheerful racket sounded good.

Then I saw the house and stopped short in astonishment. It looked like a different place. The broken windows were all fixed, and though some of the house was still that worn, weather-beaten gray, most of it had been freshly painted, in a shade of banana yellow so bright that it hurt my eyes. A ladder stood against the wall, with brushes and paint cans scattered beside it, as if whoever was painting the place had stopped in the middle and gone inside for a rest.

Even the yard was different. The tangles of bittersweet and burdock had been cleared away. A happy jumble of zinnias—red, pink, and golden—bloomed along the porch, and garden tools leaned haphazardly against the wall. Standing among the zinnias was a plywood cutout of the red-and-white polka-dotted rear end of a fat lady bending over, and there was a gigantic orange plastic butterfly fastened to the porch. Out in the yard more flowers bloomed, and a pink flamingo balanced on one foot near a line of yellow ducklings following a white mother duck, all made of plastic.

"Duckies!" shouted Amy in delight, tugging at my hand.

"Somebody's living here," I said in amazement. "But who on earth would want to live in the witch house?"

"Witch house!" echoed Amy happily. "Witch house, witch house, witches!"

"Shush," I said to her nervously. "Somebody might hear

you. And it isn't really a witch house, anyway, Amy. There are no witches."

Of course there are no witches, I repeated silently to myself. And even if there were, a witch wouldn't paint her house yellow and make such a cheerful mess out of her yard. Would she? But the house looked awfully strange, half of it still raggedy gray and half of it that crazy yellow. I couldn't help thinking of a witch in disguise. I shivered.

"Come on, Amy, let's get down to the pond," I said, and tugged at her hand. But Amy tugged back.

"Duckies!" she wailed. "I want to see the duckies!"

"No, Amy, come on, please," I insisted, glancing nervously at the gaudy yellow house, as unexpected as the blare of a radio on that quiet hilltop. I hoped whoever lived there wasn't peeking at us through the windows. Amy came reluctantly along, still looking wistfully back over her shoulder at the plastic ducklings.

I was relieved to see that the hay field beyond the house still looked the way it always had. A farmer from down in the valley mowed it every year. Joe and I used to come and watch the huge tractors and baling machines roar around the field, turning the grass into sweet-smelling bales of hay.

But today the field was quiet and empty. A short way across it, I could see the reeds and willows that marked the edge of the pond. Amy pulled her hand free and took off ahead of me, running eagerly in her sturdy pink sneakers. But I didn't have any shoes on, and the field was newly mowed. The hay stubble poked sharply into my bare feet. I limped slowly around the edge of the field, trying to avoid the stiff stubs. By the time I reached the back of the field, where the glitter of water appeared like magic among the reeds, Amy was already running along the bank of the pond, caroling one of her noisy songs. Red-winged blackbirds flew, scolding, out of the reeds, and scared frogs splashed into the water.

"Don't fall in!" I shouted anxiously, starting to run after her.

Amy stopped short. "I won't fall in," she reassured me. "Don't fall in," she ordered her bunny. She turned away from the water and began yanking up black-eyed Susans by the heads.

Well, at least she had obeyed me, I thought, dropping breathlessly onto a big rock under a willow tree by the water's edge. I had only been keeping up with Amy for half an hour, and already I felt worn out. Maybe this summer was going to be more work than I'd expected. Anyway, for the moment she was quiet.

I had always called the rock I was sitting on my dreaming rock. In the willow's shade by the quiet water, it was a perfect place for thinking. I closed my eyes and tipped my face toward the sky. Blackbirds called overhead. Water whispered at the edge of the pond, and wind rustled in the willow leaves. I could smell pond mud and newly cut hay.

I wondered why Aunt Kate hadn't told me that somebody was living in the witch house. Maybe she didn't know. She and Amy had gotten to the cabin only the day before I had, and if they had come after dark, they wouldn't have found out. Thinking of Aunt Kate reminded me, with a little twinge of guilt, of the fib I'd told her. I sighed.

If only I weren't so boring. If I were more interesting— more talented, like Joe, or more beautiful, like Aunt Kate, or more *something*—I wouldn't have to make up things like that.

I remembered the name I'd invented for myself that morning—Alexis Deveraux. Somebody with a name like that would be pretty, with long legs and long black hair, just like Aunt Kate's. And she'd be good at something, too. Not basketball or computers; something artistic, with a name like that—dancing, or painting, or writing. All three—why not? If I were Alexis Deveraux, I would be a creative genius, I decided.

Sometimes, lately, I had started telling daydreams like these to other people as if they were the truth, the way I had told Aunt Kate about the fake art prize. The day before, for instance, on the Greyhound bus that had brought me to Binghamton from Massachusetts, I had sat beside a nice, white-haired lady knitting a sweater. She kept asking me about myself, and finally I had told her that I was an only child and that I lived in New York City, in a penthouse, with my mother and father, who were both famous artists. I told her about how we traveled all over the world, and how I modeled for their paintings, and how they didn't believe I should go to school because it would stifle my creativity.

None of it was true, of course. But it all sounded so much better than the boring reality. And while I was making it up, I almost believed it myself. It was a real shock when the bus stopped and the knitting lady said good-bye, and I saw Grandpa waiting for me in the Binghamton rain and remembered who I really was.

A mosquito bit my ankle. I slapped it and opened my eyes, thinking that Amy had been quiet a long time. The pond glittered, the reeds nodded in the breeze, the blackbirds soared—but where was Amy? I couldn't see her among the reeds, or beside the pond, or in the black-eyed Susans.

"Amy?" I called. "Hey, Amy, where'd you go?"

But nobody answered. Anxiously, I stood up. She wasn't in sight in the hay field. She couldn't have fallen into the pond, I thought—I was sitting right there, and I would have heard the splash. But where was she?

I ran into the hay field. The stubble jabbed into the soles of my feet, but I hardly noticed.

"Amy? Amy! Where are you?" I yelled. How could she have dropped out of sight so fast? I tried not to think of the woods all around the edges of the field, stretching over the hills for miles in every direction. My heart began to pound with a heavy, sickening slowness. Amy couldn't be lost, she just couldn't be. Where would I go, I asked myself frantically, if I were three years old?

Then I thought I heard a snatch of one of her songs, floating across the hay field from the direction of the witch house, back by the road. Was it her voice, or had I imagined it? Maybe she'd gone back there to look at those plastic ducklings she had wanted to see when we walked past. That had to be it. Not letting myself think about any of the other, more awful possibilities, I hobbled on my bare feet straight across the stubbly hay field toward the house, as fast as I could limp.

I was already yelling, "Amy! Where are you?" as I ran on sore feet into the softer grass of the yard. But there was no sign of Amy among the ducklings and the zinnias. I glared suspiciously at the fake flamingo. "Where's Amy?"

I demanded. But the flamingo didn't answer. There was no escaping it; I had to go up to the door.

I hesitated on the witch house steps. Whoever lived here couldn't be a witch, I told myself again. I'd never heard of a witch with a pink flamingo in her yard. Anyway, witches or not, I had to find Amy. I ran up the steps, crossed the creaky porch to the door, and knocked.

It must not have been closed tightly, because it swung open promptly under my fist. The first thing I saw, in the dimness beyond the door, was Amy, perched on a chair, clutching her bunny and a cookie. She looked up at me and grinned, with a mouth full of crumbs. "I didn't fall in!" she boasted, rather thickly. "I have a cookie!"

"Oh, Amy!" I ran across the room and hugged her, cookie, bunny and all. "You scared me half out of my wits!"

"And what about you, young lady, frightening me?" demanded a voice behind me.

I swung around, letting go of Amy. In my relief at seeing her, I had forgotten to worry about witches. But there, framed in a doorway, was an old woman in a black dress that fell to the floor. Her white hair flared out around her head in a wiry mane, and she was scowling at me out of strange, very pale eyes that seemed almost to see through me. Her bony right hand was pointed accusingly in my direction, and her left clutched the handle of a broom.

3

I stammered something, grabbing Amy's hand. It flashed through my mind that perhaps I should take the cookie away from Amy—what if it was enchanted? But before I could move, another woman bustled in from the doorway behind her.

"Here, child, I found the kitty to show you—" she was saying. Then she saw me. "My goodness, another one!" she said, and beamed at me with a wide, sunny smile that reminded me somehow of Amy. Though she was as old as the witch woman, who was still glaring at me, the two were as different as a chicken is from a crow.

The lady in black was stiff and bony, but the one with the cat was on the plump side, comfortable-looking, like a couch. She had on a pink-and-white flowered shirt over orange pants, so bright she almost vibrated when I looked at her. But at least her clothes weren't witches' robes. And the cat in her arms wasn't a black, spooky-looking witch's cat, either. It was just an ordinary fat orange tabby cat that looked as if it wished she would put it down.

Now that I looked around, I could see that I wasn't in a witch's parlor. The room was a cheerful jumble. An elegant antique couch with newspapers strewn all over it stood beside a pair of folding aluminum lawn chairs. The bookcases were overflowing with paperbacks and piles of gardening magazines, and an ornate mahogany table was cluttered with trowels, spilled sacks of potting soil, and flowerpots. All the windows were jammed with plants—blooming geraniums, hanging ivy, so many pots full of leaves and flowers that the light in the room was dim and green.

The room was too untidy and colorful to be exactly restful, but it wasn't spooky. Even though nothing matched, everything seemed to go together and to go with the plump lady with the cat in her arms, all colorful and shabby and cheerfully messy. Everything, that is, except the crow lady, who stood in the middle of it all, dark and bony and as out of place as a shadow.

"Were you looking for this baby?" clucked the plump lady. "You must have been worried!"

"Well, I was," I said gratefully.

"I saw her in the yard," she said. "She was too little to be out alone, so I brought her in. I knew somebody must be with her somewhere nearby. I was just about to go outside and see."

"We were down by the pond," I explained. "I think she wanted to look at the—um—stuff in your yard."

The plump lady beamed. "Oh, does she like my garden? My sister doesn't approve, of course, but I've had fun with my flowers and my decorations since we moved in."

The crow lady snorted. I turned to her and said, "I'm sorry if I startled you, running into your house like that. I was scared when I couldn't find Amy."

"Hmph. Well, I suppose that's all right." The crow lady was glaring rather nervously at Amy. "I don't see very well, and I suppose I am easily startled. If I frightened you, I apologize. But you must understand, I am not accustomed to children."

27

"You two must be sisters, just like us." The plump lady beamed fondly down at Amy.

"No, Amy's my cousin. I'm taking care of her this summer for my aunt. My name is—" I hesitated. I was tempted to say that my name was Alexis Deveraux. I could tell them that I was an orphan, and that a plane crash had killed my parents and my brother, but I had miraculously survived, and I was living with my aunt and studying to be an artist . . . but the crow lady was staring straight at me with those odd pale eyes. Her face was fierce, and for a moment I thought she could see right through my eyes and read everything I was thinking.

"My name is Alice," I said. "Alice Dodd."

The crow lady just kept glaring at me, but the other lady said, "Welcome to the Bird House, Alice Dodd, and—did you say Amy? Amy, too." She set the fat cat gently into Amy's arms. Amy sat down happily on the floor and started singing loudly into the cat's ear.

"Um—the Bird House?" I asked. "We always called it the witch—I mean—" I stopped in confusion, but the plump lady didn't seem to notice.

"Oh, yes, it was always called the Bird House when we were girls, because our last name is Bird," she said. "When we came back up here to live last spring, I thought it would be nice to use the old name once again."

"You used to live here?"

"Yes indeed, this was our father's house, and we grew up here. It's been empty since he died, years ago now. My sister and I have lived together down in Binghamton for a long time. We always dreamed of coming back here, but we never could find the money to repair the old place until this year. But now I have my pension, and—"

The crow lady snorted again. "Abigail, you are chattering again, and we have not introduced ourselves. Child, this is my sister, Miss Abigail Bird, and I am Merlina Bird. You may call me Madame Merlina. That is my spirit name." She held out a bony hand toward me.

I thought I must have misunderstood her, so I ignored the part about the spirits. I took her hand awkwardly, not knowing if she wanted me to shake it or kiss it or what. It felt like a bundle of sticks. "Um, nice to meet you, Madame —um—Madame Merlina. And you, too, Miss Bird."

The plump lady was still smiling down at Amy, who was feeding bits of her cookie to the reluctant cat. "Please call me Miss Abby; that's what the children where we used to live always did. It's so nice to see children again. This house gets so dull with just us two old ladies in it."

Madame Merlina snorted again. "Kindly speak for yourself, Abigail. I am not old, and I do not find this house dull. I appreciate the quiet here. It is favorable to the spirits."

She certainly looked old to me. What spirits? What was she talking about? I glanced nervously at Amy. She had finished her cookie, so if it had been enchanted, it was too late now. But before I could ask Madame Merlina what spirits she meant, Amy got up, dumping the cat out of her lap, and trotted across the room, reaching toward something on a table beyond some curtains in a shadowy alcove. "Ball!" she cried suddenly, and grabbed at it.

"Put that down, child!" Madame Merlina leaped forward in a swirl of black cloth and snatched the object out of Amy's hands. Startled, Amy burst into tears.

"Oh, Merlina, you've made her cry!" Miss Abby hurried over to Amy.

"I had no intention of making the child cry," retorted

the crow lady. "But my crystal ball is no toy for a small child, Abigail."

Miss Abby was patting Amy and cooing to her. "Would you like another cookie?" she said, and Amy's crying stopped as if someone had turned off a faucet.

"Okay!" she said.

"Wait," I said. "Maybe we ought to get home."

"Won't go home!" Amy exclaimed. "I play with kitty. I want another cookie. Another cookie, please?" She smiled hopefully at Miss Abby, and I burst out laughing in spite of myself.

"Oh, won't you stay a little while?" Miss Abby was already hurrying toward the door to what must be the kitchen. "Sit down, sit down. We've been so lonely up here. I could give you some lemonade, and maybe you'd like a cookie, Alice—"

It was too late to argue; she had disappeared into the dim depths beyond the doorway, and Amy had skipped after her, chattering busily about how her bunny needed a cookie, too.

Madame Merlina was carefully placing the sphere of crystal back onto its carved stand. I followed her into the alcove and peered at it curiously. It looked like the snow globe Grandpa kept on his desk. But Grandpa's snow globe had tiny figures of children inside, building a snowman, and if you shook it a snowstorm whirled merrily around. There didn't seem to be any children, or soap-flake snow, inside this one. It couldn't be a real crystal ball, of course, not the kind in stories. But what was it, then?

The alcove where Madame Merlina stood looked very different from the rest of the cluttered, cheerful room. It was darkened by a dusty, plum-colored velvet curtain pulled partway across the door, and the furniture in it was dark and heavy, unlike the bright, shabby stuff in the rest of the room. Two big carved wooden chairs were pulled up to the table where the crystal ball stood, and beyond that was a glass-fronted cabinet crowded with old books and odd-looking objects I couldn't quite see in the gloom.

Madame Merlina seemed to be ignoring me. She sat down stiffly in one of the carved chairs, picked up a deck of cards, and began to lay them out on the table, peering at them through a magnifying glass. Somehow they didn't look like ordinary cards. I leaned closer, trying to get a better look at them. They didn't have the ordinary hearts and spades on them. Instead, there were elaborate little drawings, each one different. A lady in a long white dress bending over a lion, a child riding a horse under a blazing sun, and—what? I drew back in disbelief. A skeleton, riding a horse, carrying a black flag and glaring out of the picture, straight at me.

I couldn't help wondering if I should have taken the cookie away from Amy, after all. And just as I was wondering, Madame Merlina looked abruptly up at me and demanded, "Child, are you a medium?"

"What? I mean, no, I wear small, usually," I stammered in confusion.

"No, no, I am not referring to your clothing size," she said impatiently. "A *medium,* I said—a person in contact with other worlds. I meant, are you in touch with the spirits? Have you encountered the extraordinary?"

"Well, no," I answered hesitantly. "At least, I don't think so—"

"Well, what are you waiting for?" interrupted the old woman. "Come over here and sit down." Her pale eyes were fierce. It didn't occur to me to disobey.

As I sat down nervously in the other chair, she put the cards and the crystal ball aside, took a flat wooden box out of the cabinet, and opened it. Inside it lay a polished wooden board, hand-painted with the letters of the alphabet and the words *Yes* and *No* in old-fashioned, curly script. Ceremoniously, Madame Merlina set the board on the table between us. She took a tiny, carved ivory triangle with a hole in the middle and legs like a little table out of the box and set it in the center of the board.

"Have you ever seen a Ouija board, child?" she asked me.

I shook my head. "I've never even heard of one. What is it?"

Ignoring my question, she rested the tips of her withered fingers on the little triangular table. "Place your fingers lightly on the planchette," she directed me. "Exactly like mine. Good. Now, concentrate. Let the spirits flow through your fingertips."

"Wait a minute," I blurted out. "What is this thing for?"

As soon as the question was out of my mouth, the little table she had called a planchette began to slide under my fingertips, tugging my hands gently along with it the way the undertow tugs at your feet at the seashore. It slid across the board to the letter *I* and paused there for a moment. I glanced at Madame Merlina, thinking that she was pushing it. But her sour old face was fixed on the board, and her fingertips seemed to be barely resting on the planchette. If she was pushing it, I couldn't tell.

"What does it say?" she croaked impatiently. "I can't see

very well without my glasses, child. Read the letters out loud."

"*I,*" I read obediently, my voice squeaking a little, and the planchette began to move again, swinging over to another letter as purposefully as if it were alive. I read each letter out loud as the planchette paused over it, and Madame Merlina repeated the letters after me.

"*I . . . S . . . E . . . E*—I seek . . . *T . . . R . . . U . . .* truth!" she said, as the sliding planchette came to a stop. " 'I seek truth.' Well! I must say, that is not what I expected. You must be a very spiritual child. I shall ask the spirits about you."

She paused for a moment and cleared her throat. "Oh, spirits, we greet you," she said, in a different, deeper voice, sounding a little eerie, like someone in a horror movie. "Is this child an old soul? What was she in her last incarnation?"

Under my fingers, the table slid again, like magic. It slipped across the board to the word *Yes.* Then, as if it were alive, it took off again, down the board to the letter *O.*

"Read me the letters, child," insisted Madame Merlina. "Weren't you listening?"

"Oh, sorry," I said. "Let's see, *O . . . W . . . L . . .* " The little planchette skidded from letter to letter so quickly that I had to concentrate to keep up.

"Owl!" exclaimed Madame Merlina. "In a past life, child, you must have been an owl!"

I yanked my fingers away from the little table as if it had burned me, glaring suspiciously at Madame Merlina. Owl! How could she know about my awful nickname from school? Kids at school had called me Owl, or sometimes even Owly Alice, all year. And it wasn't just because of the terrible owl picture I'd made for the contest. It was also because I looked like an owl. My glasses made my eyes way too big, and my hair, as I said before, was kind of feathery, and—well, what with one thing and another, I was a little sensitive about that word. Angrily, I slapped my fingers back onto the planchette.

I didn't intend this part of it, honestly. It was an accident. But when my fingers landed on the planchette, it slid a little way across the board, stopping over the letter "A."

Madame Merlina didn't seem to realize that I had accidentally pushed the planchette. She squinted at the board.

"Is that an *A?*" she murmured questioningly. "Owl-a? Perhaps that is a name. Perhaps I was mistaken, and we have made a contact." She paused and cleared her throat. "Spirit? Spirit Owla, are you with us?"

Some kind of spirit got into me at that point, though probably not the kind Madame Merlina had in mind. This time, very gently, I pushed the planchette on purpose. It resisted just a little at first. But I pushed a bit harder, and under the pressure of my fingers, it slid obediently on its felt feet, straight across the board to the word *Yes.*

Madame Merlina glanced up at me, her face delighted and unexpectedly young-looking. "Why, we've contacted a spirit! Spirit—Owla—who are you?"

I stared back at her for a moment, trying to figure out whether Madame Merlina really believed what she was saying. She couldn't, I told myself. It was just too weird. She had to be joking, just as I was. But that mischievous impulse was still in me, and I thought I might as well see how far I could push the joke. Madame Merlina repeated her question.

"Who are you, spirit Owla? Are you—are you female?" It was easy to push the planchette once again, back over to the word *Yes,* and from there to one letter after another, reading the letters out loud as I went, to spell out the words *Princess Owla.*

"A princess! Princess Owla," repeated Madame Merlina, in an awed voice. "Princess Owla, where is your kingdom?"

By this time I was ready to giggle, or make the board spell a rude word, or somehow bring the joke to an end. But Madame Merlina wasn't. She repeated the question, and then repeated it again, her voice growing stern. I looked at her fierce face with those bristly eyebrows, and suddenly I was afraid to tell her I'd been fooling her. What would she do if she got angry? What if—I looked again at that long black dress and the strange pale eyes—what if she really was a witch?

"Where is your kingdom?" demanded the old woman again, and suddenly I remembered Aunt Kate, back at the cabin that morning, telling me about the mythical island of Atlantis. Quickly, I pushed the planchette around the board once more.

"*A-T-L-A-N-T-I-S.*" I read the letters out loud.

"Atlantis?" repeated Madame Merlina. "How remarkable! Princess Owla, of lost Atlantis!" Her bony hands on the planchette were trembling with excitement. "Abigail!" she cried, as her sister, carrying a tray loaded with glasses of lemonade and a plate of cookies, came back into the room with Amy, who left a trail of cookie crumbs behind her. "In a previous lifetime our guest was a princess of lost Atlantis! It was revealed to us by the Ouija board!"

Miss Abby seemed to flinch a little, but then she smiled sunnily and set the plate of cookies down beside the board. "Oh, Merlina, are you still playing that silly game? Stop now and have a cookie, won't you?"

"I've told you before, Abigail, it is not a game." Madame Merlina's voice was as sulky as a child's. Miss Abby just kept smiling and said nothing.

I took my hands off the planchette with relief and nibbled on a cookie. It didn't taste enchanted; it seemed to be an ordinary oatmeal cookie, with raisins in it.

Madame Merlina seemed to forget her irritation. She scooped up a cookie and ate it in a couple of excited bites. "A sensitive!" she exclaimed, swallowing the cookie. "Child, you must be a sensitive, an open channel to the spirit world. You are a medium, just as I suspected!"

I wasn't at all sure I liked the sound of that. But just then Amy, trying to reach another cookie, got hold of the tablecloth instead and yanked it off the table. Madame Merlina grabbed the crystal ball in time, but the Ouija board, the planchette, and the plate of cookies tumbled around Amy, who started to wail. Miss Abby picked everything up and I tried to comfort Amy, but Madame Merlina just sat there scowling at us and didn't help at all.

I found Amy's bunny under the table and gave it to her. She clutched it and stuck her thumb into her mouth, and her crying subsided into sniffles and gulps. "I'd better take her home," I said, lifting Amy into my arms. "I'm sorry about the mess."

"Oh, don't worry about it, dear, she's just a baby. Please

come see us again soon. I'd love to show you my garden," said Miss Abby.

"Come back tomorrow," ordered Madame Merlina. "We have work to do together in the spirit world." Amy was clutching my shirt with cookie-crumb-covered fingers. Madame Merlina eyed her with distaste. "Couldn't you leave that child at home?"

"Oh, Merlina, don't be so rude!" exclaimed Miss Abby. "Alice, child, come back whenever you want to, and of course you must bring Amy, too."

I said good-bye and escaped with Amy into the crazy yard. My stomach hurt a little. Sometimes it did when I made things up. It was silly, I told myself, to feel bad about tricking Madame Merlina. She was a grown-up, after all. She must have known I was faking it.

But before I'd gone more than a few steps, I realized that my feet hurt more than my stomach did. I set Amy down. Balancing myself on the plastic flamingo, I stood on one sore foot and lifted the other to look at the bottom. It was a mess of small cuts and scratches from running across the hay field when I couldn't find Amy.

I'd managed to forget all about losing her, but I could see that my sore feet were going to remind me of it for a while. Next time I'll keep a better eye on her, I promised myself as I limped after Amy down the lane toward the cabin. And I'll wear my sneakers, too.

4

When we got back to the cabin, Aunt Kate was standing on the porch, frowning. She had pinned up her hair into a knot at the back of her head, making her look older and more severe.

"There you are!" she exclaimed when she saw us. "I was just starting to wonder if I should worry."

"Mommy!" Amy yelled. She wiggled out of my arms and ran up the porch steps. "I saw duckies, Mommy!"

"Duckies? Wow! Lucky you!" Smiling at Amy, Aunt Kate picked her up. Then she looked at me over her head, and the smile faded. "Where did you go, Alice? I was kind of anxious."

"Just up to the pond," I said uncomfortably. "Amy wanted to play outside, so we took a walk. I didn't know you would worry. I'm sorry."

"Well, that's okay, I guess." Aunt Kate carried Amy down the porch steps into the yard. She still wasn't really smiling. "But I'd rather you didn't go to the pond by yourselves. And I'd like to know where you are, okay? So I know where to look for you, if I have to."

"Okay, sure." Staring down at my feet, I dug a hole in the sand of the lane with my scratched, sore big toe. It was only my first day as Amy's baby-sitter, and already I was doing things wrong. Of course I should have told

Aunt Kate where we were going. What would she say when she found out that I had done such a bad job of watching Amy that I had almost lost her? At this rate, Aunt Kate was going to be sorry she'd ever hired me for the summer.

Amy was bouncing up and down in Aunt Kate's arms, hollering, "Duckies! Duckies! Duckies!"

"Oof," said Aunt Kate, struggling to hold on to her. "Okay, okay, tell me about the duckies. Did you see duckies at the pond?"

But Amy just kept bouncing and yelling, so I explained.

"We didn't see real ducks. She's talking about some fake ducks in the yard up at the witch house—I mean, that old farmhouse by the pond. Somebody's living there."

"Oh, that's right. Your Grandpa mentioned that last night." Amy was still wriggling and yelling, and Aunt Kate set her down, watching as she ran off across the yard to the sandpile under the beech tree. "He said he hadn't met them yet, but he'd heard they were from the family that lived there when I was little, when Grandpa first built the cabin. Did you see them?" Aunt Kate turned to me, her smile friendly and curious again.

"Yes, we did. We met them, in fact," I said, relieved that she seemed to have forgiven me. "They're two old ladies. Sisters, they said. One of them is named Abigail Bird. She said to call her Miss Abby. And the other one is named—um, Miss Merlina Bird." I hesitated over the crow lady's name. I couldn't bring myself to tell Aunt Kate that she had told us to call her Madame Merlina. It just sounded too peculiar.

"That's right, their name was Bird. I remember now."

Aunt Kate raised an inquisitive eyebrow. "Well, what did you think of them? Grandpa said he'd heard down at Davenport's that they're a bit odd."

Davenport's Market was a little store in the village of Muskrat Falls at the bottom of the hill. Mrs. Davenport, who ran the store, kept an eye on everything that went on around town, and talked about it to everyone who came in. Grandpa had always said that he could learn more about life from spending an hour at Davenport's than he could from reading the newspapers for a week.

"But if the Bird family still lived here when you were little, don't you remember them?" I asked.

"Not really. We were only here in the summers, you know, and I was pretty young. They closed up the place and moved out only a year or two after Grandpa built the cabin. From what Grandpa said, he never got to know them, either."

"Why not?" My grandpa is the type of person who usually gets to know everyone; he likes to talk to people, and most people like to talk to him.

"I guess they kept to themselves. I think Mr. Bird was a bit of a tyrant—he was the father of these ladies you met today, I think. I only saw him once, but I still remember it." Aunt Kate gestured toward the end of the lane. "Your mom and I were playing near their house, and he came stomping out in his bathrobe, yelling about all the noise we were making. He had all this wild white hair, and bristling eyebrows, and very strange, pale, scary-looking eyes. And he was carrying a big stick. We ran back to the cabin—we were so scared! It wasn't too long after that that he died, and they left. I think the whole family was kind of—well, eccentric, you might say."

I shivered. Aunt Kate's description of old Mr. Bird sounded exactly like Madame Merlina. I remembered the way she had glared at me out of those strange pale eyes when she ordered me to sit down and use the Ouija board. *Tyrant* was the right word for her, all right.

"So what are these two sisters like?" asked Aunt Kate. "I know I'm being nosy, but are they as odd as Mrs. Davenport says?"

"Well, they were kind of weird," I admitted.

"Weird how?" Aunt Kate frowned again. "Maybe you and Amy should keep away from there. At least until I meet them."

"Well, they both wore kind of peculiar clothes. And they're painting the house bright yellow, Aunt Kate. It looks like a school bus or something. And there are all these corny garden ornaments outside. A pink plastic flamingo, and fake ducks, and all kinds of strange stuff."

"That doesn't sound so bad." Aunt Kate grinned wickedly. "I always wanted to put a pink flamingo in the yard here, but Dad wouldn't hear of it."

"Aunt Kate!" I was startled at the idea of changing anything at the cabin. To me, it looked perfect just the way it was.

"Oh, come on, Alice, you're as bad as your grandpa. It would be funny. Where's your sense of humor? Anyway, I'm glad somebody's sprucing up that house. It was always such a spooky old place. I used to be scared of it, you know, when I was your age. I thought it was haunted. I'd run past, especially at night."

"*You* were scared?" I gazed at my grown-up, confident aunt, struggling to picture her as a girl my age, as scared of the witch house as I was. I couldn't do it. "I used to be

41

scared of it, too," I admitted, careful not to mention that even this morning I had been glad to hold on to Amy's hand as we walked past the house.

"Oh, the place terrified me." Aunt Kate grinned at me, her blue eyes so sympathetic that I suddenly wanted to tell her all about what had happened with Madame Merlina that morning. I had the oddest feeling that Madame Merlina hadn't been pretending—that she had really believed that we were speaking to the spirit of a dead princess named Owla who had lived in Atlantis. It didn't seem possible that a grown-up could believe a thing like that. But Madame Merlina had acted so excited, just as if she did believe it. And besides, the Ouija board had seemed to really move, when we first sat down, before I pushed it. How could it have? Maybe Aunt Kate could help me figure it out.

"Aunt Kate," I began. "Did you ever hear of something called a Ouija board?"

But Aunt Kate had stopped listening to me. "Watch out, Amy, don't fall!" she called. Amy was just pulling herself up into the lowest branch of the beech tree. Aunt Kate ran across the yard, ducked through the leaves, and put a hand on Amy to steady her.

By the time she had turned back to me, I was hesitating. Maybe I shouldn't tell her, after all. What if she didn't understand? What if she thought it was a bad thing to do, trying to trick an old lady? Maybe she wouldn't understand that I had never expected Madame Merlina to believe me.

Before I could decide, Aunt Kate spoke. "Alice, I know what I forgot to tell you," she said. "Grandpa's coming to dinner tonight. He called while you and Amy were out.

We'll have to run down to Davenport's. I've got chicken and potatoes, but there's nothing for dessert."

That good news drove Madame Merlina and her Ouija board right out of my head. Even though I had just seen Grandpa the night before, I was always ready to see him again. "Aunt Kate, can I bake him a blueberry pie, please?"

"Well, sure, if you want to," said Aunt Kate. "But do you know how?"

"Yes!" I said. "Grandpa taught me."

I really did know how to bake wonderful blueberry pie. There was a big patch of wild blueberries in the woods not far from the cabin, and every summer we picked quarts and quarts of them. My grandmother used to make blueberry pies and blueberry muffins, and she always froze lots of berries for the winter. After she died, my mom and Grandpa kept it up, and they taught me. We used Grandma's pie recipe, with lime juice instead of lemon, and her special flaky crust. That pie always tasted to me like summer, like Grandma's sweet floury hugs, like the cabin on a hot August day—like home.

"What a great idea," said Aunt Kate. "Maybe you could teach me how. I'm a lousy cook. I'm not sure I've ever made a pie. Certainly not a good one, anyway."

"As long as there are blueberries in the freezer, I can," I said confidently.

"Why can't we just pick some?" asked Aunt Kate.

"They aren't ripe yet. They don't get ripe till later in the summer," I explained. "But usually Grandpa keeps some frozen."

"I've been living in the city too long, I guess." Aunt Kate lifted Amy out of the tree. "I can't keep track of things like that. Anyway, if you want to bake a pie, that would be wonderful. Then we won't have to go down to the store." Aunt Kate's pinned-up hair caught on one of the low branches of the beech tree as she and Amy ducked under it. Impatiently, she pulled the hairpins out and shook her head to free it, and her black hair fell down loose around her shoulders. There were spatters of blue paint mixed with the freckles on her cheekbones, and with her bright eyes and her raggedy jeans, she didn't look much older than I was as she and Amy came toward me, hand in hand, across the yard.

"You remind me of your mom, did you know that?" she said. "When we were kids, she could do all those competent things, like baking pies. I was always burning them or putting salt on the berries instead of sugar. I think after a while your grandma just gave up on teaching me."

As I hobbled on my sore feet across the grass Aunt Kate stopped suddenly and frowned at me. "Alice, you're limping! What did you do to your feet?"

"I scratched them," I admitted reluctantly. "Amy and I walked across the stubble in the hay field, and I didn't have my shoes on." I shoved my hands into my pockets unhappily, remembering all of a sudden that I had hurt my feet by running across the field in a panic when I couldn't find Amy. We had been having such a good time talking about pie that I had forgotten that I still had to tell Aunt Kate about that. I wished I didn't have to. What if she got mad at me again?

"Goose," said Aunt Kate. "Why didn't you go around the edge?"

I took a deep breath and opened my mouth to explain

exactly why I'd been in too much of a hurry crossing the field to go around the edge, but Amy interrupted.

"Mommy, stop talking!" she shouted. "I want some lunch!" I couldn't believe she was still hungry after all those cookies, but Aunt Kate laughed.

"Okay, okay. We'll have to do some work on your manners sometime, but for now, peanut butter and jelly, coming up," she said, and the two of them headed for the kitchen.

I did find a few packages of last summer's blueberries in the freezer, so after lunch Aunt Kate and I got out the rolling pin and the pie pans and went to work, while Amy enthusiastically "helped."

Baking a pie with a three-year-old is quite an experience. It took about twice as long as it would have if I had done it alone, what with Amy dumping a whole cup of salt into the pie crust and then spilling most of the berries and squashing the ones she tried to pick up. By the time the pie was safely stashed in the oven at last, all three of us were covered with flour, and Amy had so much blueberry juice on her face and hands that she looked like a little bouncing blueberry herself.

A couple of times while we were making the pie, I tried to tell Aunt Kate about losing Amy. But it was a hard thing to do. Every time I opened my mouth to say something about it, my hands would sweat and my heart would start to pound, and I'd close my mouth again. "Later," I'd promise myself. "I'll tell her later."

But we were busy all afternoon, making the pie, and keeping track of Amy, and cleaning up the mess in the kitchen afterward, and I never found the right moment.

Somehow, the longer I waited, the harder it got to explain about losing her, or even worse, to explain why I'd waited so long to tell Aunt Kate about it.

And so I didn't get around to telling Aunt Kate about losing Amy. I really didn't have to tell her about it. Or at least, that's what I told myself. It wasn't that important. Amy hadn't actually gotten lost, after all. I had found her right away. And anyway, if I told Aunt Kate about losing Amy after already not telling her where we'd gone that morning, I'd be in trouble all over again. And it wasn't as if anything bad had happened, I told the nagging voice in my head. It didn't matter if I told Aunt Kate or not.

5

Aunt Kate put the chicken in the oven to roast and took Amy away to give her a bath before Grandpa came, while I finished wiping flour off the countertops. Listening to Aunt Kate and Amy singing in the bathroom on the other side of the closed door, I began to feel a little lonely. I wished Chloe was around, or Karen, or somebody my age. I had hoped maybe I'd get a letter from Chloe that day, but there had been nothing for me in the mail. Much as I liked Aunt Kate and wanted to know her better, in a way it was going to be a lonely summer, with nobody around but a grown-up, a wild three-year-old, and some very peculiar neighbors.

At least Grandpa was coming. He was due to arrive any minute, and he was always good company. I decided to go outside and watch for his car.

Outside, I wandered over to the beech tree. It was a wonderful tree, with spreading branches that reached almost to the ground so that in the shade of the translucent green leaves, I felt as if I were in a glimmering private world.

I ducked under the low branches. In the sandpile where Amy had been playing before lunch lay a bent teaspoon that she must have been using for a shovel. I picked it up and squatted to dig aimlessly in the sand. When we were younger, Joe and I used to spend hours in this sandpile.

And after we got too big for that, we used to pretend that the tree was a fort, or a spaceship, or whatever else we thought up. We'd climb around in the branches all afternoon, sighting enemies in the distance or warning each other of approaching meteor showers. I sighed. I was too old to play those pretend games anymore, of course. But sometimes I wished I still could.

I stuck the spoon in my pocket, stood up, and swung myself up onto the lowest branch of the beech tree. The silvery bark was smooth and a little slippery. It was an easy tree to climb; the branches grew in exactly the right places for a climbing person to put her hands and feet.

I scrambled quickly halfway up the tree, wincing only a little as I climbed on my scratched feet. I peered down the valley, looking for the dust from Grandpa's car climbing the dirt road that led up the hill from Muskrat Falls. I couldn't see anything, so I climbed higher, and then still higher, watching the road through the branches. The tree rocked a little in the breeze, like a ship.

I am a sailor, I thought, climbing in the rigging of a ship. I climb higher and higher, searching the horizon for land. We have been lost at sea for days. We are starving and almost out of water. I must find land and save us all.

I climbed higher in the tree, deep in my daydream. I am at the top of the rigging now, in the crow's nest. I can see for miles over the shining sea. I can see dolphins leaping, and a whale spouting foam, and—there! Far in the distance, the hazy shape of an island, the land we have been searching for. It is Atlantis! We are saved!

"Land ho!" I shouted.

There was a sudden rustle and a clatter beneath me as something slipped from my pocket and tumbled through the branches. I squinted down through the leaves. It was the spoon I had picked up in the sandpile, lying far below me on the ground. Very far below me. All of a sudden I swayed and clutched at the skinny branches around me. I hadn't realized how high I had climbed. I was almost at the top of the tree, higher than I'd ever climbed before. The branches up here looked too thin to hold my weight. I swallowed, wedged one foot between two thin limbs, and stared straight ahead of me at the narrow trunk. Somehow, I had to climb back down. But how could I do that if I couldn't even look below me without getting sick?

Time seemed to stop while I was in that tree. I couldn't move. Every time I looked down into the branches and saw the truth of just how high up I was, I got dizzy again and had to close my eyes. My fingers seemed frozen to the smooth bark of the branch I was clutching, and my knees wobbled so much that I was afraid they would shake me right out of the tree. I thought of yelling to Aunt Kate for help, but when I opened my mouth, the only sound that would come out was a croak.

I thought I would cry with relief when I finally heard the crunch of tires on the sandy lane, the slam of a car door, and Grandpa's rumbling bass voice singing something I was too frightened to recognize.

"Grandpa!" My voice croaked again, but I forced it out. "Help!"

Grandpa stopped singing. "Is there a bird in the beech tree? Must be a big one!" he exclaimed. I could hear footsteps rustling through last year's fallen leaves. They stopped directly underneath me. "Aha!" he cried. "It is a bird! It's a brown-tufted granddaughter! Wish I had my binoculars for a closer look. Planning to fly down?"

"Grandpa, stop it," I wailed. "It isn't funny. I can't get down! You have to help me!"

"Help you! I can't fly up there and get you, Alice. I'm no bird." The laughter still filled Grandpa's voice.

"I can't climb down, Grandpa. I'm stuck up here!" My voice was getting thinner and higher. The smooth beech bark slipped under my sweaty fingers. "I'm afraid to look down!"

Grandpa was quiet for a minute, and when he spoke again, he wasn't laughing anymore. "Okay, honey." His sudden seriousness made me feel a little better. "Hang on," he said. "I'll get you down."

His footsteps rustled away. I kept my eyes squeezed shut, but I heard the screech of the shed door opening, a dragging sound, and some thumps. After a few minutes, Grandpa's voice floated up to me again, puffing a little, sounding closer. "Haven't climbed up here in years," he said. "Think I'm getting too fat for it." I hazarded a quick, dizzy glance down. A ladder was leaning against the cabin and Grandpa stood on the flat roof below me, his bald head shining, still lower than I was, but much closer.

He gazed consideringly up at me. "Now, Alice," he said. "This is a challenge. Can you move your left foot down, just six inches, to the branch underneath it?"

"No!" I closed my eyes again and clutched the branch tighter.

"Come, come," said Grandpa. "That doesn't sound like the Alice I know. Where is your spirit of adventure?"

I didn't answer. Grandpa was quiet a minute. Then his voice floated up again. "I seem to recall that Bilbo Baggins walked right into the dragon's cave, even though he was afraid. If a little hairy-footed hobbit can be brave, so can you. Right?"

Even through the tears of panic beginning to sting my eyes, I had to laugh. The summer before, Grandpa had read me *The Hobbit*. I remembered how Grandpa read, waving his hands, jumping up sometimes to stride around the room. June bugs had banged against the screen as if they wanted to hear the story, too. I remembered Grandpa's rumbling, comfortable voice, and the wood-smoke smell of his old corduroy jacket, and the way the firelight glinted on his glasses.

And all of a sudden I found I could move my left foot, and there was a branch six inches below it, just as he had said. And then I moved my right hand where he told me to, and found another solid branch. And then I moved my other foot, and then my left hand, until little by little, I climbed down the tree, relying on the steady tones of Grandpa's voice directing me, as if the familiarity of it were the solid earth itself beneath my feet. And finally I was on the ground again, knees still shaky, and Grandpa's round face was beaming at me as he climbed down the ladder from the roof.

"I'm glad you did that, Alice in Wonderland," he said. "Otherwise I would have gone to my grave never knowing I'm still young enough to climb up on that roof. Now, let's go have supper." He took my arm, and we went inside.

Supper that night was a noisy affair. Amy, of course, talked without stopping, and Grandpa and Aunt Kate talked almost as much as she did. I didn't say much; I didn't have to. The other three kept up such a constant stream of songs, stories, and general nonsense that all I had to do was sit there in the middle of it and watch them eat my pie, which was delicious in spite of Amy's help.

Aunt Kate was talking about an ad campaign she had just finished the illustrations for in New York. "Dancing tomatoes they wanted me to draw, Dad," she said, shaking her head. "Four years of art school and all these years of work so that I could grow up and paint pictures of dancing tomatoes."

"Doesn't seem right, does it," said Grandpa sympathetically, but his blue eyes were twinkling at Aunt Kate. "I'll bet you paint a bang-up dancing tomato, though, Katie."

Aunt Kate's eyes twinkled back in just the same way. "I do the best dancing tomatoes in New York City, Dad—that's why they came to me," she said. "It's a relief, anyway, not to have to do any ad work this summer."

"Want to show us the painting you're working on now?" asked Grandpa.

I looked up eagerly. The door to the sun porch where Aunt Kate's painting things were had been closed since I arrived, and I was curious. Except for a portrait of me and Joe as babies that hung over the mantel back home in Massachusetts—and the ads and cereal boxes, or course— I'd never seen any of Aunt Kate's work.

"Sure," said Aunt Kate carelessly. "Come take a look."

We followed her out to the porch. There were tubes of paint and rags and brushes scattered on the glass-topped table where Grandma used to serve iced tea, and several untouched canvases were propped against the wall. Aunt Kate's easel stood in the corner, and Grandpa and I trooped past her to peer at the half-finished painting on it.

It was a watercolor, all in blues and greens, the outlines wavery and vague. There were curving shapes in the background that might have been hills or waves, and glimmering columns that could have been pillars or seaweed, and in and out of the columns moved long green shapes that looked like horses, or maybe dolphins. Dancing through the middle of the painting was a girl in a flowing robe, long hair floating out behind her. Everything was hazy, as if the land Aunt Kate had painted were already underwater. It was as vague and beautiful, as impossible and also perfectly right, as one of those dreams that you hate to wake up from, that you try to remember but can't quite, that haunt the edges of your thoughts all day. I drew in a shaky breath, staring at the painting, and let it out again. I could think of nothing to say that was beautiful enough for that picture.

Grandpa didn't have my problem. "Well, Katie," he said, "That'll beat a dancing tomato any day. Doesn't look much like Plato's Atlantis, though, does it? Ought to be walls in concentric circles, and towers, and lagoons, as I remember my Plato."

"Plato invented his Atlantis, Dad," said Aunt Kate mock-severely. "I invented mine."

Grandpa put an arm around her shoulders. "Don't get prickly, Katie. I like your version better than Plato's any day." He reached down to pick up Amy, who was hopping beside him on one foot, and showed her the picture. "Are you proud of your mommy? You ought to be."

"Fishies," caroled Amy. "Lotsa fishies. Grandpa, I wish I was a fishie, and I'd swim in there and sing all day."

That's more or less what I was wishing. I couldn't tell if the picture was supposed to show Atlantis before or after it sank below the sea, and I didn't care. Wherever it was, it was the most beautiful place I had ever seen. My body was still on the porch, staring at the picture. But my mind was far away, in the kingdom of Atlantis, where I danced dreamily across that blue-green land, my gauzy purple robe flowing around my feet, the princess Owla of Atlantis, before it was lost.

"Alice likes to draw, you know, Dad," said Aunt Kate suddenly, and I snapped out of my dream. "Sounds as if she's pretty good. She said she'd do some drawing for me, when we get a chance."

Grandpa peered at me over the top of his glasses. "That right?" he said. "Never knew you were an artist, Alice. Thought you were just a bookworm, like me."

"Oh, I can't really draw much," I stumbled, hoping Aunt Kate wouldn't mention the stupid contest prize I'd invented. If I had ever really won a contest, I would have called Grandpa to tell him right away, and he knew that, so he would know I'd made it up. "I'm—I'm just learning, really."

"Good!" said Grandpa. "One fool artist in the family's enough, anyway, don't you think, Katie?" Grinning his wide, teasing, I-don't-mean-it smile, he reached out and ruffled Aunt Kate's shiny black hair. She crossed her eyes and stuck out her tongue at him, and then she grinned and put an arm around him. I let out a sigh of relief as the two of them went back to the living room together.

I stood there another minute, gazing at Aunt Kate's picture. I wish I could paint like that, I thought wistfully. I wondered about that dreamy girl dancing across the painting. I bet *she* never got into trouble making things up. I bet she never worried that she wasn't pretty enough, or popular enough, or talented enough. She was perfect just the way she was, dreaming and beautiful, dancing as if that was what she was made to do. I pushed a hand through the short brown tufts of my hair and sighed. Why couldn't life ever be the way it was in books and pictures? Why were real things so hard?

6

I think I dreamed, that night, about Aunt Kate's painting. When I woke up the next day, those dreamy images were still swimming around in my mind. I wanted to look at the picture again, but right after breakfast Aunt Kate went out to the sun porch to work, closing the door behind her.

Amy didn't get upset when the door closed this time. She was wearing shorts and a T-shirt with three yellow ducklings on the front. That reminded her of the plastic ducks at the Bird House, and she sang about duckies and waddled around the cabin quacking while I finished up a piece of leftover blueberry pie. Pie has always been one of my favorite breakfasts.

When I'd eaten the last crumbs, I stood dreaming at the kitchen window, watching the way the light drifted green through the beech leaves like the oceany light in the painting. I didn't know Amy had gone outside until I saw her through the window, trotting across the yard.

"Hey! Wait up!" I banged through the kitchen door and ran after her. "Amy, where are you going?"

Amy smiled sweetly back over her shoulder. The sun made a halo out of the fine curls on top of her head. "I go see the duckies," she said. "You come, too."

"You have to stop running off without me," I panted. Or I had to learn to keep a better eye on her, I thought uncomfortably. But I couldn't watch her all the time. How did mothers do it, anyway?

"Wait a minute, Amy. I have to tell your mom where we're going." Amy came cheerfully enough back to the cabin with me. I tapped on the sun porch door and called to Aunt Kate that we were taking a walk up to the neighbors' house. "Okay." Her voice drifted through the door, sounding a bit vague and distracted. "Don't be gone too long."

I took Amy back outside, holding her hand firmly so that she couldn't get away again, and we started up the lane toward the Bird House. My feet felt much better today, hardly sore at all. The day was cloudy and hot, and the trees were a duller, darker green than they had been in the sunshine the day before.

But the Bird House, when we got there, was as loud a shock of banana yellow as ever. As we came past the pine trees, Miss Abby straightened up from a flower bed and waved a trowel at us, looking, in red polka-dotted stretch pants and an enormous turquoise T-shirt, like one of her own lawn ornaments come to life.

"Good morning, dears. You're just in time to help me bed petunias," she called.

Amy ran right up to her. "Quack," she announced. "I'm a duckie."

"So you are, dear," agreed Miss Abby amiably. "Would you like to help me dig?"

Still quacking, Amy took the trowel out of her hand and got busily to work, sending up showers of dirt like a chipmunk.

"Alice, dear, look on the front porch where the gardening things are, would you please?" asked Miss Abby. "Somewhere up there you'll find a statue of an owl. I want to put it in this flower bed to scare off the birds from eating my plants. But I don't want to haul this big fat old body up those steep steps. Lord, it's hot." She wiped her forehead with a red bandanna, and Amy wiped her own hand on her forehead in careful imitation.

I crossed the yard and climbed the steps into the cool shade of the porch. Behind me, Amy and Miss Abby were chattering to each other in their light, twittery voices, so much alike that they sounded almost as if they were the same age.

One end of the porch was piled high with a jumble of tools, flowerpots, and more lawn decorations. I rooted around in the clutter, looking for the owl. There were plywood ducks with wings that would rotate in the breeze, birdhouses, tulips cut out of wood, and a windmill showing Uncle Sam milking a cow with the words *U.S. Taxpayers* painted on her sides. I couldn't imagine where Miss Abby had gotten all that stuff. If she put all of it out in the yard, the place would look like a circus.

In the jumble I found an owl, scowling accusingly out of empty plastic eyes. I held it up and studied it critically. Made of drab beige plastic, with rough grooves to indicate wings, feathers and beak, it didn't look much like an owl. It wasn't any better than the awful drawing I'd made in school, I thought. I didn't think it would fool any real birds for a minute.

Unexpectedly, a deep voice spoke behind me. "Good morning, child."

I turned around quickly, clutching the owl. Madame

Merlina stood in the doorway, dressed in weird black clothes just like the ones she'd had on the day before. "I am glad you have come," she said formally. "I would like to explore the Ouija board further with you. It is not at all unusual for the spirits to respond strongly to a young girl like yourself. I have already prepared the board for another session with you."

"Well—um—" I stammered, edging past her toward the steps. "I don't think I can do that today. I have to take this owl to Miss Abby, and I do have to watch Amy, you know."

But Madame Merlina took the owl out of my hands. "Nonsense," she said. "The child will be perfectly all right with Abigail. This is an important matter, after all." She raised her voice. "Here is your statuette, Abigail," she called. "Alice will be indoors with me for a time. You can supervise that child, I assume."

Miss Abby smiled at us over her shoulder from the petunia bed where she and Amy knelt side by side. Their two back ends looked cheerful and homey somehow, Amy neat in her little yellow shorts and Miss Abby bulging in polka dots. I wished I could stay outside in the bright garden with them.

"Of course," she said, her round face broad and comfortable in the sunlight. "Amy and I are doing fine here. You go ahead inside, Alice, and visit. Don't worry about us, child. Run along."

Madame Merlina set down the owl at the top of the steps and turned toward the house. I shrugged helplessly and followed her inside, where the plants in the windows made the light dim and green and watery, like Aunt Kate's painting of Atlantis. I'd just have to tell Madame Merlina I wouldn't do it, I told myself. I didn't want to fool around about Atlantis. Somehow, after seeing Aunt Kate's painting, Atlantis didn't seem like a joking matter to me anymore.

Madame Merlina marched straight across the living room to her dark alcove, where she already had the Ouija board set out, with a candle in a tall bronze candlestick burning beside it.

Then she gestured, like a queen, at the chair where I had sat the day before. "Sit down," she ordered me. "Let us begin."

I stared at her unhappily. I knew what I had to do: Open my mouth, right then, and explain to her that I had only been fooling around the day before, that I had invented Princess Owla, that I had pushed that planchette. The longer I waited, the worse it would get, just as the longer I had put off telling Aunt Kate about losing Amy, the harder that had become.

I cleared my throat. "Madame Merlina, I have to tell you something," I said.

"Hush, child," she said impatiently. "Unnecessary chatter will destroy our concentration. Sit down."

"But, Madame Merlina—" I tried again.

"Silence!" she snapped, her pale eyes blazing. "Child, do not argue. Do as I say!" She pointed at the chair, her old hand shaking.

Fury welled up in me. What a bossy old lady, I thought angrily. If she won't listen when I try to tell her the truth, it serves her right if I lie. I sat down hard in the chair and pulled it up to the table with a jerk.

Madame Merlina didn't seem to notice my indignation.

She settled herself in the other chair, her back straight, her wrinkly hands planted firmly on the planchette. She sat still for a moment with her eyes closed, and then she spoke. "Spirit Owla!" She was using that low, spooky voice again. I thought she sounded ridiculous. "Princess Owla, spirit from Atlantis, will you speak with us today?"

Still hot with anger, I didn't hesitate. I wiggled the planchette from side to side for a moment, as if the spirit of Princess Owla were slowly waking up. Then I pushed it across the board to the word *Yes* and read it aloud.

"Ah!" Blinking, Madame Merlina sat back a little. "You have returned! Princess Owla, will you—ahem—will you answer our questions?"

Maybe in broad daylight I wouldn't have dared to go any further. But I was annoyed enough at Madame Merlina, just then, to be meanly glad that she couldn't see very well. In that dim room, by the flickering candlelight, I knew she wouldn't be able to see the small movements in my fingers as I pushed the planchette around to the word *Yes* again.

Madame Merlina took a deep breath, as if collecting herself. "Well, then," she said. "Please, Princess Owla . . . tell us about Atlantis."

I pushed the planchette from letter to letter, reading each one aloud. "*I-S-L-A-N-D,*" I spelled.

"Yes, yes, we know that," said Madame Merlina eagerly. "But was it—was it beautiful?"

I pushed the planchette back to *Yes* one more time. Madame Merlina said nothing, waiting, as if she expected more.

Wondering what else to say, I looked past her, out of the dark alcove where we sat to the green planty light in the living room. I wasn't so angry anymore. But as I thought about Atlantis, my mind was filling with the dreamy image of Aunt Kate's painting. It was so beautiful, that world she'd painted, so green and shimmery. "G-R-E-E-N," I made the Ouija board spell, and I relaxed a little, letting myself be caught up in the memory of the painting and the enchanted way it had made me feel. "G-R-E-E-N H-I-L-L-S, G-R-E-E-N W-A-V-E-S," I spelled, reading each word slowly as I spelled it. "G-R-E-E-N O-C-E-A-N W-O-R-L-D."

As I pushed the planchette around the board, I had to speak slowly, one word at a time, so that I didn't get ahead of the Ouija board. Talking that way felt like walking through deep water, the way it drags and holds you back so that you can't hurry even if you have to. The candle flickered in the dark room and the planchette swooped across the board under my hands, back and forth in a sleepy rhythm. Although I knew the sun was shining outside, Madame Merlina's parlor was as gloomy as nighttime, and I felt almost as if something magic really were happening, as if I were under a spell. I forgot I was making it all up. I just daydreamed aloud about the magical country in Aunt Kate's painting, and as I daydreamed, it all seemed real.

"H-A-L-F L-A-N-D, H-A-L-F S-E-A," I chanted slowly as I slid the planchette around. "G-R-A-S-S W-A-V-E-S, C-L-O-U-D S-H-I-P-S. B-I-R-D-S F-L-Y L-I-K-E F-I-S-H."

What I was spelling out didn't seem to make much sense, even to me. But Madame Merlina sighed. "It sounds beautiful." Her eyes were closed, and she was speaking just as slowly as I had, her voice dreamy.

I was still seeing Aunt Kate's painting, and that young

girl dancing across it with her hair afloat. *"A D-A-N-C-E-R F-L-O-A-T-S,"* I went on, pushing the planchette from letter to letter. *"D-A-N-C-I-N-G O-N W-I-N-D, O-N S-E-A."*

It was easier to use the Ouija board if I left out the little words, like *the* and *and*. And it gave the story I was inventing a poetic feeling, so that it had a magic of its own. I could almost feel myself dancing slowly across the rippling grass, the warm wind lifting my hair, as long and silky as Aunt Kate's, my robes swirling in the breeze.

"Who is the dancer?" asked Madame Merlina, her eyes still closed.

"I am," I said dreamily, and I almost let my hands stop moving. But as I spoke, I remembered just in time that I had to push the planchette. I shoved it quickly around the letters *I A-M,* glancing nervously at Madame Merlina. But she didn't seem to notice.

"You dance, Princess Owla?" she asked, her voice still dreamy, her eyes still closed. "A dancing princess. How lovely. Is it a—ceremonial dance? A ritual of some kind?"

Why was she dancing, that mysterious girl in the picture? Not for a ceremony, not because she had to. She danced for the joy of it, because dancing was what she was meant to do. I thought of a line of poetry my mother liked to quote, and as soon as I thought of it, I was spelling it out on the board.

"H-O-W S-H-A-L-L W-E K-N-O-W T-H-E D-A-N-C-E-R F-R-O-M T-H-E D-A-N-C-E?" It was the longest sentence I'd spelled out. I read the words as I went, and stopped, a little breathless, as I finished pushing the planchette around.

I smiled down at my fingers, pale and dim in the can-

63

dlelight, like pebbles underwater. I was as pleased with the beautiful dream I was weaving as if a real spirit had created it. I didn't know what the poetry meant myself, but it sounded wonderful.

I guess Madame Merlina thought so, too, because she opened her eyes and stared at me for a moment without saying anything. Then she cleared her throat as if getting ready to ask another question.

But before she could, the porch door flew open with a bang that made me jump, and Amy ran in, with Miss Abby bustling behind her.

"What are you two doing in here in the dark?" Miss Abby asked, flicking on a light. "It's so stuffy in here. Wouldn't you like a cool drink?"

Amy scrambled up into my lap, knocking the Ouija board askew. "Alice, we planted flowers," she squealed in her most earsplitting voice. "And we planted an owl, too, right in the middle of the flowers!"

Madame Merlina let out her breath in an exasperated snort. "Abigail, you and this child have entirely destroyed our concentration. You have no respect for the spiritual at all. You are every bit as silly now as you were when you were a girl."

"I suppose you're right," said Miss Abby cheerfully. "I'm sorry, Merlina; we didn't mean to interrupt your game. But don't you want some lemonade, anyway?"

"It is *not* a game," said Madame Merlina icily. "And no, I do not want any lemonade. I simply want to be left alone. Is that really too much to ask?" She blew out the candle, slapped the Ouija board back into its box with a bang, stood up, and stomped out of the room.

"Oh, dear." Miss Abby looked after her ruefully. "Merlina is so touchy about this silly spirit business. I don't know why she takes it so seriously. She ought to come out in the fresh air once in a while and forget about all these old spooks of hers. Ah, well, she'll get over it, I suppose. Now, Alice, *you'll* take a cold drink, won't you?"

I nodded, smiling weakly, as Amy slid down from my lap and ran after Miss Abby into the kitchen. But I didn't follow right away. I sat still in the heavy carved chair, glad to be alone for a moment. Though the room was hot and stuffy, I felt chilled and a little dazed, as if I were coming out of a trance.

Somehow, the story I'd made up had taken on a life of its own. It had felt almost as if there had been some real enchantment at work, I thought, some kind of magic. Of course, I knew there hadn't really been any magic. My own hands and my own imagination were the only forces that had moved that planchette. But I didn't know who was in control anymore, me or my fantasy. And sitting there staring at the blown-out candle, I felt a little scared.

7

Aunt Kate was still painting in the sun porch when we got back. We could hear her singing through the closed door, an old English folk song about lost love. I knew the song because my mother liked to sing it, too. Their voices were a lot alike, clear and pretty. But somehow, Aunt Kate made the song sound sadder.

She wasn't sad when she came out, though. She picked Amy up, whirled her around and hugged her, and she beamed at me and said that her painting was going beautifully and that she had me to thank, for doing such a good job of watching Amy. I gulped, remembering that I still hadn't told her about losing Amy the day before. Maybe it would be okay just to forget about it, I thought. After all, everything had gone fine today.

There was still no letter for me from Chloe, but I did have a letter from my mother, which she must have written right after she put me on the bus to come to the cabin. The letter was short, cheerful, and busy-sounding, just like my mother. Most of it was about things I already knew—my father's vegetable garden and Joe's plans to go to Cape Cod with his girlfriend's family—so it wasn't very interesting. Halfway through the letter, I found my mind on Madame Merlina instead of on what I was reading.

I still felt a little creepy about that morning's Ouija board session. Madame Merlina really did seem to believe in the princess Owla, and in Atlantis. And the scary part was that, for a while there this morning, I had, too.

I'd just have to stay away from the Bird House, I told myself. I wouldn't go near the place. That way, Madame Merlina couldn't make me do the Ouija board again. And sooner or later, she'd probably forget about it. At least, I hoped she would.

After lunch, Amy took a nap, and Aunt Kate and I went outside to lie on towels in the sun. She was still in a good mood, talking to me about her painting and the ad agencies she worked with and what it was like living in New York City. It was nice on the warm grass, with a light breeze blowing over us and making the pine trees rustle, and at first I just lay on my stomach and enjoyed the warm sun soaking into my back. But after a while I started to feel a little uncomfortable about Madame Merlina again. Maybe I should try once more to talk the whole business over with Aunt Kate.

"Aunt Kate." I rolled over to stare up into the blue depths of the sky. "Do you know anything about Ouija boards?"

"About what?" Aunt Kate's voice was drowsy and contented.

"Ouija boards," I repeated. "Um—talking to spirits. Things like that."

Aunt Kate thought about it for a minute. "I've never used a Ouija board, but once in high school a friend of mine read my Tarot cards."

"What are those?"

"Cards that supposedly tell the future. You lay them out

in a pattern, and you're supposed to be able to see in the cards a person's fortune, what will happen to them, who they'll fall in love with. Things like that."

Suddenly I remembered the strange cards Madame Merlina had been studying before she got out the Ouija board. "Do Tarot cards have weird designs on them?" I asked. "Lions, and skeletons, and hung men—kind of spooky pictures?"

"That's right." Aunt Kate propped herself up on her elbows and lifted her hair off her neck.

I wondered if Madame Merlina had been reading my fortune. I wondered what the cards had said about me. "Well, did it work?" I asked. "I mean, did they really tell your future?"

Aunt Kate made a wry face. "Well, as I recall, I was supposed to make a journey to a far country and fall in love with a tall dark stranger."

"Hmm." I thought about that for a minute. Uncle Tony had been short and blonde, and I didn't think Aunt Kate had ever traveled much. I thought it was too bad, though. It would be nice if Tarot cards could tell fortunes and Aunt Kate really did fall in love with a tall dark stranger. Aunt Kate was so pretty, and she had to be a little lonely, living by herself with Amy the way she did. Then I sat up, suddenly excited.

"Well, maybe it just hasn't come true *yet*, Aunt Kate. Maybe you're still going to travel and meet a tall dark stranger and fall in love. Maybe you shouldn't give up hope!"

Aunt Kate was laughing at me. "The eternal optimist, that's you, Alice," she said. "I'm glad you think there's still hope for me."

"But don't you *want* to fall in love, Aunt Kate?"

Aunt Kate's smile changed a little. She paused a moment, running a length of her hair reflectively through her fingers. "You know, that's not an easy question," she said finally. "Right now, I'm not really sure I do."

I didn't know what to say to that. I thought everybody wanted to fall in love. That's how it seemed with my friends, anyway. Aunt Kate sat up abruptly.

"Let's talk about something else," she said briskly. "I keep forgetting that I want to see your artwork, Alice. I'm excited about that contest you won. Are you sure you didn't bring any of your pictures along?"

Although the sky was clear, the day seemed to dim suddenly, as if a cloud had covered the sun. I had completely forgotten about telling Aunt Kate that I had won that stupid art contest.

"Um, no," I mumbled. "All I brought was clothes and books." It was the truth, but somehow it felt like another lie.

"What medium do you like to use?" asked Aunt Kate.

"Medium?" I stared at her in confusion. The only medium I could think of was Madame Merlina.

Aunt Kate nodded. "You know, what medium do you work in? Pencil, crayon, watercolors?"

Now I understood. Aunt Kate meant the kind of medium artists use, not the kind who talked to spirits. I stammered, "Um, I did the owl picture for the contest with markers. I—I really haven't used watercolors much." For once I was telling the truth, anyway.

"Want to try using mine?" suggested Aunt Kate. "I'd really like to see your work."

I wrapped my arms protectively around my knees.

"Some other time, okay, Aunt Kate? I can't today—I have to, um, write a letter to my friend Chloe."

"Right now?" Aunt Kate got up, slung her towel over her shoulder, and smiled back at me as she started toward the cabin. "Well, some other time, then. But don't forget, okay? Maybe we could do it after supper."

I wrote a very long letter to Chloe that afternoon, even though really it was her turn to write to me. And after that, I wrote one to my friend Karen, visiting her father in California, and then I wrote one to my mother and father. That evening while Aunt Kate put Amy to bed, I kept the letters in my lap, rewriting things that I'd already written, keeping the pencil moving so that Aunt Kate would think that I was too busy to draw. I felt as if I were holding my breath all evening, and when she finally sat down in Grandpa's rocking chair across from me, I stared at my letter without looking up, afraid to meet her eyes in case she remembered to ask me to draw her a picture.

But she didn't say anything at all. I could hear the rocker creaking gently back and forth, but I couldn't tell what she was doing. The silence lengthened. Finally I couldn't stand it anymore. I glanced up to find Aunt Kate staring straight at me, with an odd, serious look on her face.

"Hmm," she said thoughtfully. She was frowning. Had she figured out that I had told her a fib, just from looking at me sitting there on the couch? I stared back at her in alarm and started to say something.

"Don't move, Alice," she said quickly, rummaging in the canvas bag beside her on the floor. "Just—don't—move for a second—there it is!" She fished out a sketchbook and opened it up. "Do you mind just sitting still like that for a few minutes while I draw you?" She was already making quick lines on the paper. "There's something about the way you're sitting—I just want to try . . ." Her voice trailed off.

Relieved, I sat carefully motionless, my face lifted toward her, listening to the busy scratching of her pencil on the paper. It was hard to sit perfectly still, and the longer I sat there, the harder it got. Trying not to move made me feel as if wiggling my hand or moving my head was all I wanted in the world. My back itched, and my foot was falling asleep. I couldn't help squirming just a little.

"Hold still just one more minute, Alice," Aunt Kate muttered. "I'm not done yet—can you lift your chin up just a little?"

I did. For some reason, the pose made me feel like a princess. Maybe Aunt Kate was drawing me because she needed a princess for one of her paintings, I thought, and I would be the perfect model. Maybe in her drawing I would look like a princess.

I thought of that girl in the Atlantis picture, dancing dreamily in her purple robes, so beautiful and otherworldly. Would she make me look like that? I am the princess Owla of lost Atlantis, I thought. I could imagine myself in flowing purple robes; I could almost feel the weight of a crown on my head. I stretched my chin up a little higher and tried to fix my mouth in an imperious princess smile.

Unexpectedly, Aunt Kate giggled. "Alice, what an awful face. Do you need to scratch or something?"

"No, no, I'm okay," I said hastily. I quit smiling like a princess. I could almost feel the robes dropping away and the crown falling off my head.

"Well, just say so if you need to take a break." Aunt

Kate was scribbling again. "That's much better. You look comfortable again. That's it, Alice. Just be yourself."

Be yourself, be yourself, I thought, and I could feel exasperation welling up. People were always saying "Be yourself," as if that were a simple thing to do. Be myself, indeed. How could I be myself if I had no idea who I was?

"There." Aunt Kate held the drawing away from her and studied it critically for a second, turned away from me, so I couldn't see it. "Yup, all through. Thanks, Alice. You can move now. Want to see?"

"Yes!" I hopped up eagerly. But I had forgotten about the foot that had fallen asleep. When it hit the floor, my leg buzzed as if I had stepped into a nest full of bees. "Ouch!" I hollered. I stumbled against the coffee table, grabbed at a floor lamp to keep from falling, and knocked it over.

"Ow, ow," I wailed, hopping on the good foot and trying to keep the buzzing one from touching the floor. Aunt Kate dropped the sketchbook and came over to me.

"I'm sorry. I made you sit still too long," she said remorsefully, putting an arm around my shoulder. "Is your foot okay?"

"Oh, it's fine. I think I broke the lamp, though," I said grumpily. The foot was coming back to life now, sending electric zaps up my leg. I put it down gingerly onto the floor and picked up the lamp. The bulb wasn't broken, but the shade was squashed flat on one side. Some princess, I thought bitterly. I couldn't even cross a room without destroying it. I hobbled over to the sketchbook and picked it up.

I don't know what I was hoping to see. Somehow I guess I had hoped that, through Aunt Kate's eyes, I would look—I don't know—magical. I thought I might see my-self, in her drawing, in a way I'd never seen myself before.

But that isn't what happened. There was my plain old face, staring back at me out of the sketchbook exactly the way it stared at me out of the mirror every morning. Big owly eyes, glasses crooked on my stubby nose, feathery hair, stupid-looking hopeful smile. Some princess, I thought bitterly. No tall dark stranger was ever going to fall in love with me, that much was certain.

Aunt Kate had come up beside me. "What do you think?" she asked.

"Umm . . . well . . . It looks just like me. I mean, it's a very good drawing, I guess. But . . . Aunt Kate, is this all?"

"All?" Aunt Kate took the sketchbook out of my hands and looked at it. "This is you, Alice. It's a pretty good likeness, if I do say so myself. What do you mean, all? What more did you want?"

"I don't know." I scowled at my ordinary self in the drawing, plonked on the ordinary couch with an ordinary expression on my face. "Something—different. Some-thing special. I don't know how to explain."

"You reminded me of your mother all of a sudden," said Aunt Kate, smiling at the drawing. "Sitting there scribbling away, just the way she used to. She was always writing something or reading something, just like you. And you look so much like her, Alice, do you realize that?"

"Yes, I do," I said shortly. Some princess, I thought again. Amy called out from her crib in the other room just then, and Aunt Kate handed the sketchbook back to me and went in to check on her, leaving me standing there with the drawing in my hands.

My ordinary face stared up at me from the sketchbook, my eyes peering at me through my glasses as if they expected something wonderful. I let out my breath in a snort and slapped the sketchbook face down onto the table so that I wouldn't have to look at myself anymore. Be myself, indeed, I thought glumly. Alice Dodd, princess of lost Atlantis. Phooey.

8

To my relief, Aunt Kate said nothing more about my artwork that night. The next morning, after she went off to
paint, I took Amy out into the yard. She had her duckling
shirt on again, and I guess it reminded her of Miss Abby
and the Bird House.

"Let's go see the duckies," she asked me hopefully.

"Not today," I said quickly, remembering my decision
to keep away from Madame Merlina and the Bird House
for a while. It would be fun to go up to the pond, if Aunt
Kate would let us. But keeping away from Madame Merlina meant keeping away from the blackbird pond, too,
because we couldn't get there without passing the Bird
House.

"Where could we go?" I asked myself out loud. "I know,
Amy, I'll show you the Indian trail. Come on!"

"Okay!" To my relief, Amy promptly forgot about the
ducklings and followed me cheerfully.

I headed in the opposite direction from the Bird House,
toward a path into the woods that Joe and I had always
called the Indian trail. You could follow that path through
the woods for miles, all the way down the hill to the train
tracks that ran through the village. Joe knew a lot about
the Seneca Indians who had lived in those hills before the
Europeans came, and he used to like to pretend that Senecas

had made the trail, though we both knew it probably had really been made by modern-day deer hunters.

We used to pretend that we were Senecas, following the trail to our summer hunting grounds, and Joe would dictate everything we did so that it would be just the way he thought the real Senecas would have done it. He'd make me gather herbs and roots for medicines and food. Of course, we didn't really know which plants were herbs and which were plain old weeds. We'd just gather up armfuls of sumac and goldenrod and pretend that we knew what we were picking. Or we would both work on passing soundlessly through the woods so that no twig cracked under our feet. I got pretty good at it, and it was easy to believe I was a Seneca, slipping beneath the trees on silent moccasins.

But Amy would have made a terrible Seneca. She kept up a constant chatter as she followed me into the woods, stopping every few seconds to show me a flower or exclaim over a mushroom. I've always liked to be quiet in the woods, but I didn't get annoyed by Amy's racket. She sounded almost like a bird herself, twittering away, and she tucked one small warm hand into mine so trustingly that I couldn't tell her to be quiet. This time, I decided, we weren't Senecas. We were running away. I was the big sister, and we were escaping from an orphanage, and . . .

"Oooh!" Abruptly, Amy let go of my hand and grabbed me around the knees. "I saw a monster!"

"You saw a what?" I tried to pry her loose from my legs. "What do you mean, a monster?"

Amy squinched her eyes shut and pointed blindly behind her. "Under there! A big monster! It wants to eat me up!"

I looked where she was pointing, at an ordinary-looking

rotten log lying by the path. Under some fallen leaves beside the log, something tiny rustled. I bent over Amy, who was still hanging on to my knees, and lifted up the leaves.

"It's a salamander!" I exclaimed. "Amy, don't be scared, it won't hurt you. Look, it's beautiful."

Amy loosened her grip and looked doubtfully over her shoulder. I squatted down beside her and lifted the leaves away from the tiny animal. The salamander was only a few inches long, and it really was beautiful, glossy black, with a row of glowing yellow spots down each plump side, and small, bright eyes glittering like jewels. It crouched still in the leaves, probably hoping that if it didn't move, we wouldn't see it.

"Monster's pretty," Amy said, reaching for the salamander.

"Don't touch!" I warned her. "Grandpa says you can tear a salamander's skin just by touching it. And it's not a monster, anyway. It's a salamander."

"Salamonster," Amy agreed, and grabbed for it. But the salamander was too quick for her. With a flick and a scurry, it was gone in the leaves. Amy let go of my hand and chased after it into the undergrowth.

I scrambled after her, jumping over the rotten log. "Hey, wait!" I caught up with her and grabbed her hand.

She wailed, "I want to catch the monster!"

"Not a monster, Amy, a salamander," I repeated. But Amy tugged at my hand.

"Let's find the salamonster, okay?" she insisted.

"Okay, okay." I shrugged and followed her under the trees, away from the path. I knew that the salamander was safe behind us somewhere, hiding under a rock or the rotten log. But I hadn't been in this part of the woods for a long time, and it would be fun to explore. Besides, there almost seemed to be a faint path here, running ahead of us between the trees. It was probably just a deer track that would wind a little way through the trees and then peter out, but I wanted to see where it led anyway.

We were still so close to the cabin that if I squinted back the way we had come, I could see the lighter area beyond the trees that was the clearing where the cabin stood. Amy scampered ahead of me and disappeared into a clump of trees.

"Oh!" I heard her exclaim again.

"What did you find, Amy, another salamonster?" I caught up with her and stopped short in surprise.

In the grove was something I'd never seen before: a log cabin, or a poor imitation of one—a ramshackle little structure of poles, half leaning against a tree. Amy stood staring at the shack in fascination.

"House!" she said, and ran over to it.

There was a kind of door—an opening in the logs, just big enough to crawl through. Amy ran through it, and I got down on all fours and scrambled in after her. The shack was not much bigger than a bathroom, roofless and full of leaves. The thin poles that made the walls were stacked on one another higher than my head, so loosely that daylight streamed in through the spaces between them.

"Wow." I crouched in the damp leaves beside Amy. "Why didn't I ever see this before? I wonder who built this place." Maybe Joe had, I thought, or maybe kids from down in the valley. Or deer hunters. Whoever built it, there was no sign that anyone had been inside it for a long time.

"It's a house for my bunny," announced Amy. She laid her bunny down and covered it with leaves, all but its face. "Bedtime, bunny," she said firmly. "Go to sleep now."

I was getting wet from sitting in the leaves. "I know what, Amy," I said, getting up and brushing off the seat of my shorts. "Let's clean up. This can be our hideout, okay?"

Amy stuck out her lower lip. "Mine," she insisted. "My bunny house."

"Okay, okay, it's your bunny house," I agreed, but I was thinking of it already as my own hideout. I could come here by myself in the afternoons, when I didn't have to watch Amy, I thought. As the two of us scooped the leaves out the door and brushed down cobwebs from the corners, I daydreamed about how I could spend whole afternoons in the hideout by myself, reading, thinking, being alone.

I broke a few branches off a pine tree and heaved them up on top of the walls so that the sweet-smelling needles made a sort of roof. Using another pine branch for a broom, I swept the dirt floor reasonably clean. We found a couple of short, thick logs and rolled them inside for chairs, and I set another one on end for a table. Amy wanted a chair for her bunny, too, so I found a smaller log and set it carefully beside the others. Amy picked some ferns that were growing under the trees and I stuck them into a rusty tin can and set them on the log table. It was surprising how nice it all looked when we were done.

"There," I said, sitting down on one of the logs and looking proudly around. "It's perfect." And it was. There was something magical about the airy little building. It was just big enough for the two of us. Sunlight dappled in through the evergreen needles and the loosely stacked log walls, and the sweet, bright smell of pine filled the hideout.

I would have liked to stay there all day, but before long Amy got hungry, and I hadn't brought anything along for a snack. There was no point in telling her that it wasn't lunchtime yet. One thing I had already learned about Amy was that when she was hungry, she was hungry, and there was nothing to do about it but feed her. Next time, I thought, as I ducked through the low door after her, I'll bring along some saltines and some apples and a coffee can to keep them in. And a gallon jug of water and some cups, and some books, and maybe some kind of rug to cover the floor, and a curtain or something for a door.

I glanced back at my hideout as Amy and I followed the deer track back through the woods. It had a homey, welcoming air, and the pine branches I'd put on top made it look, somehow, as if it belonged to me. I could hardly wait to come back.

9

I didn't have to wait long. That afternoon, Aunt Kate took us down to the village to do some errands, so I didn't have a chance to get back to the hideout. But the next day, as soon as Aunt Kate shut herself away in the sun porch, Amy and I went straight back to the hideout. I left Aunt Kate a note, as I'd promised her I would whenever I took Amy away from the cabin, but all I wrote was that we were going to play in the woods. I didn't want to tell her about the hideout. At least, not yet.

I lugged along a canvas bag full of graham crackers, a jug of water, picture books, crayons, and drawing paper to help keep Amy busy. I was beginning to learn that a lot of the secret of taking care of a small child was just being prepared.

When I got to the hideout, everything was still the way we'd left it, except that the ferns we'd stuck in the can had withered for lack of water. I dumped them outside, and Amy helped me pick a fresh bunch of ferns and orange jewelweed from a clump blooming in a patch of sun. I left Amy picking more jewelweed and took my bunch of flowers into the shack, where I put them into the can with a little water from the gallon jug.

Then I sat down on one of the logs and looked around at the rough walls and the dirt floor. I felt as proud of my hideout as if I were Princess Owla herself, looking around her castle in Atlantis. "My domain," I said out loud in a regal, Princess Owla voice.

The flowers in the rusty can looked beautiful against the rough, gray bark of the logs, the orange of the dangling jewelweed blossoms brilliant among the dark-green fern fronds. If I were Aunt Kate, I thought, I'd paint that.

I pulled the drawing pad and a pencil out of the bag, listening absently to Amy talking to herself outside the hideout. She wouldn't stay interested in the jewelweed much longer, I knew. But I probably had a few minutes of peace before I'd have to come up with something else to keep her busy.

Maybe I could teach myself to draw, I thought. At least I could get a little better at it. That way, if Aunt Kate ever remembered again to ask me to draw something for her, maybe I wouldn't embarrass myself.

I squinted at the ferns for a moment, chewing thoughtfully on my pencil. Then I began trying to trace out their feathery shapes on the paper. I remembered the way Aunt Kate's hand had danced across the paper the night she'd drawn that picture of me. She'd made it look so easy.

But it wasn't easy, of course. The shapes of fern and flower and leaf were so complicated that I couldn't make the pencil echo them. I could see how the jewelweed flowers dangled from their stems like little trumpets, but I couldn't get their beauty down onto the paper. After fifteen minutes of trying, I had a pile of false starts, each one just a few curved lines and unrecognizable leafy shapes.

I kept at it, though, even after Amy got tired of picking flowers and appeared at the door looking for something else to do. I fished a picture book out of the bag, shoved it at her hastily, and went back to my picture. I was just beginning to get it right, and I didn't want to stop. After only a minute or two, Amy demanded another book. I passed one to her out the door without even taking my eyes off my drawing. This one kept her quiet for a while, and finally I came up with a stiff, awkward picture that did look, just a little, like jewelweed and ferns in a can.

I propped the sketchbook against the wall and shook my head. The ferns were all right, but the flowers were awful. The tin can did look a lot like a tin can. But it wasn't the way I wanted it to be, and it wasn't like Aunt Kate's drawings. The shapes were wrong, and even the lines didn't look quite right. I remembered how Aunt Kate's lines swooped sure and strong across the page, but mine were rough, made of lots of uncertain, hairy-looking little marks.

For some reason I didn't feel completely discouraged. It had been fun, just trying to make the picture come out well, even though I hadn't succeeded. I gazed critically at my drawing, trying to figure out what I'd done right and how I might be able to fix the mistakes.

Then Amy appeared at the door again, holding out her book. "Read it to me, Alice," she begged.

"Okay, okay. You've waited long enough." I turned reluctantly away from my drawing and held out my arms for her to come into my lap. But as she did, she stumbled and bumped into the wall. The loosely stacked logs creaked and wobbled, and for a minute I thought the whole thing would fall on top of us. One of the pine roof branches let go and tumbled down, landing on Amy and me with a gentle ploof and a shower of pine needles.

The rest of the hideout didn't fall. But after that, I was careful not to bump the walls, and I kept Amy away from them when she was inside.

After that, I went to the hideout almost every day. Sometimes I took Amy there in the mornings, while Aunt Kate worked. But the best times were the afternoons, when Aunt Kate took care of Amy, so I could slip off alone and have the place all to myself, to draw as much as I wanted.

At first, I drew at the hideout because I was hoping to teach myself enough about drawing so that, if Aunt Kate ever remembered to ask me to draw her a picture, I could make a good one. But as the days went by and I slowly filled up my drawing pad, I forgot about Aunt Kate. I kept on drawing just because it was fun.

I had never done a lot of drawing before, except for that terrible owl picture. I'd never wanted to. I'd always felt as if somebody were looking over my shoulder, judging my pictures and criticizing them. When I did start something, I'd usually crumple it up before I'd managed more than a few lines.

But at the hideout, there was nobody to see, and I drew and drew. I drew the canful of ferns and flowers over and over again, trying to get it right. And when the flowers withered, I took the drawing pad outside. I drew the birch trees that grew in a grove around the shack, trying to show the way their white trunks stood out against the dimness of the woods. I drew a rock jutting out of the forest floor, moss covering it like a shawl, one small flower huddled against it. And once, when she sat still long enough, I drew Amy, half-asleep in a clump of ferns with her bunny in her lap.

I wasn't satisfied with any of my pictures, although I could see that they were gradually getting better. I still couldn't make my lines as sure and graceful as Aunt Kate's, and the shapes I drew were stiff and clumsy. But the more I drew, the less it mattered whether my results were what I'd hoped for. I drew just because it felt so good. Concentrating on how to draw the toothed edge of a birch leaf, I'd forget about everything else, forget about where I was, forget even who I was. And if I came up with a drawing that echoed even part of the shape of that leaf, I'd feel wonderful.

I carried the drawing pad and Amy's pile of picture books back and forth with me every day, afraid to leave them at the shack in case of rain. In the cabin, I looked carefully at Aunt Kate's drawings whenever I got the chance, studying her lines and the way she arranged things on the page and how she used shading. I hid my own sketchbook between the mattress and the box spring of my bed. And at night sometimes, alone in my room, I'd pull it out to add a little shading to a drawing, or change a line here or there, or just look through the drawings. The sketchbook began to seem to me almost like a hidden treasure.

Even though I'd started drawing in the first place to please Aunt Kate, I didn't tell her, or anyone else, what I was doing. I kept my sketchbook secret from Aunt Kate. I didn't tell my parents about it when we talked on the phone. I didn't even write to Chloe about it. I had an odd, uncertain feeling about the drawing I was doing. I was proud of my work, and I loved the way I felt while I was drawing. But I wasn't ready to show my work to anybody yet. I felt almost as if my drawings were like a new baby, or some other new, vulnerable thing that needed protection.

I didn't tell Aunt Kate about the hideout, either. I don't know why I cared so much about keeping it secret. Aunt Kate wouldn't have minded my going there. It just felt good, somehow, to have a private place that nobody knew about but me. Of course, Amy knew about the hideout, but she was really too young to count. I tried to tell her not to talk about it, but she was too young to understand. She talked a lot about her "bunny house" when we were back at the cabin. Aunt Kate didn't pay much attention; she seemed to think it was just another one of Amy's crazy made-up ideas. Once, though, I thought Amy was going to give the whole thing away.

Amy and I had spent the morning at the hideout. That afternoon, the three of us were out in the yard when Amy grabbed Aunt Kate by the hand and tugged her toward the Indian trail.

"Come on, Mommy," she said. "Come see my bunny house."

For a minute I thought Aunt Kate was going to go with her and I'd lose my secret refuge. It was strange how awful I felt, as if a hole had suddenly opened up inside me.

But Aunt Kate saved me, without even realizing it. "I know what," she said to Amy, as if she hadn't heard her mention the bunny house. "Let's go see if the blueberries are ripe."

The blueberries worked like a charm. Amy was always

eager to go anyplace where there was food. She forgot all about the hideout immediately and followed Aunt Kate happily past the pine trees at the edge of the yard to the blueberry patch, where the berries were just beginning to ripen.

Left behind, I stood smiling in the yard. In my mind's eye I could see the hideout, safe and private in the woods, still my secret. And as soon as I could, I told Aunt Kate I was going off by myself for a walk, and I went straight to the hideout to draw.

Sometimes drawing reminded me a little of the Ouija board. When I was really focused and concentrating, the pencil moved across the page almost as if it had a life of its own, as if it knew where it was going, even if I didn't. It reminded me of the way the planchette had moved on the Ouija board the first time I'd tried it with Madame Merlina, before I'd started pushing it. But drawing felt good, while using the Ouija board had ended up making me feel awful. I didn't like to think about the Ouija board. It reminded me of Madame Merlina, and I felt better when I forgot about her.

I didn't manage to forget the Bird sisters altogether, though. One afternoon, I set out for the hideout while Aunt Kate and Amy both took afternoon naps, my sketchbook and drawing pencils stowed in my bag along with some apples. I hadn't gone very far up the Indian trail when I rounded a curve and nearly fell over Miss Abby, squatting at the side of the path. In a flowered sun hat and scarlet smock, she looked wildly out of place among the soft green ferns.

Speechless, I stopped short. What could Miss Abby be

doing out here in the woods? Crouched like that, she looked almost as if she had been trying to hide. Was she spying, or lying in wait for me, or what?

But Miss Abby just glanced calmly up at me with one of her warm smiles.

"Why, hello, dear," she said, as graciously as if we had met in her parlor. "It's been so long since I've seen you. How are you?"

"Fine," I said uncertainly. "But Miss Abby, what—what are you doing here?" It sounded rude, but Miss Abby didn't look offended at all. Her rosy face still perfectly cheerful, she held up a small blue guidebook.

"I'm identifying ferns." Grunting with the effort, she struggled to her feet and showed me a picture of a fern in her book. "This clump is an interrupted fern. You can tell by the brown leaflets with the spores that interrupt the fronds in the middle of the stem, see?"

Feeling a little ashamed of my suspicions, I looked from the illustration to the fern. They did look alike, but I was more interested in the delicate, precise drawing in the book than in the plant itself. How had the artist been able to draw it so exactly? I knew from painful experience that drawing ferns was hard.

Miss Abby interrupted my thoughts. "Where's that sweet little Amy?" she asked.

"Back at the cabin. It's her nap time right now," I said.

Miss Abby smiled. Her eyes were as pale as Madame Merlina's, but in her round, rosy face, they looked warm and kind instead of strange and scary-looking. "We've missed Amy lately. And we've missed you, too, Alice."

"Um—well—um," I stammered. "We've been kind of busy."

"Of course you have," said Miss Abby gently. She watched me steadily from under the flowered brim of her sun hat, something I couldn't quite read in the expression on her kind, round face. "My sister isn't always—well, very easy to get along with, I suppose," she said. "But I think she misses you, dear."

I grunted doubtfully. Whatever Miss Abby said, I didn't believe that Madame Merlina really missed me, or anybody else. If that grouchy old woman missed anything, it was just the opportunity to boss me around and make me use the Ouija board, whether I wanted to or not.

Miss Abby kept talking. "She gets a little lonely up here, you know, even if she does deny it, and she did seem to enjoy visiting with you very much." She patted my hand with her plump, dirt-stained one. "But I should get back now. She'll be wondering where I am. I hope you and Amy will come over again soon, dear. My sister would love to see you, and so would I. Maybe tomorrow?"

"Maybe, if we can. We'll see," I agreed reluctantly, and Miss Abby waved a cheerful goodbye as she went off down the Indian trail toward the lane, pausing here and there to examine a plant. Relieved, I stood and watched her go, as out of place in her bright clothes among the quiet green pines and birches as a large, lost, tropical bird.

In spite of my promise, Amy and I didn't go to the Bird House the next day, or the day after that. Instead, we went to the hideout almost every morning, and whenever I could I went back by myself in the afternoon. I didn't just draw when I was there. Sometimes I read, or I wrote letters to Chloe or Karen or my family. And sometimes I just sat, listening to the small sounds of the woods and watching the green light sift through the pine-needle roof.

But not long after the day I met Miss Abby, I was doodling in my sketchbook one afternoon, daydreaming, not really thinking about what I was drawing. After a while, I looked at my own moving fingers to see with a shock that what had emerged on the page was a frowning face with wild hair, bushy eyebrows, and pale eyes that seemed to stare right through me. My picture looked so much like Madame Merlina that it scared me. I flipped to a new page, quickly, to cut off her accusing gaze—but not before I had noticed that there was something in the way I had drawn her eyes that looked a little sad.

10

In the beginning of August, I woke one morning to the sound of rain on the roof. It was the first rainy day since we'd found the hideout. While Aunt Kate painted and Amy watched cartoons, I prowled restlessly around the cabin.

What I wanted to do was draw—I could feel my sketchbook tugging at me, like a magnet, from its hiding place under my mattress. But it didn't feel right to draw in the cabin. And in the rain, I couldn't get off by myself, and I couldn't get to the hideout. I felt restless and cranky, as if I had poison ivy.

Amy was restless and cranky, too, and before long, she got bored with the television. She fooled around with toys halfheartedly for a few minutes. Then she got up and went over to the sun porch door.

"Mommy?" she called through the door. She tried to open it, but the old door stuck shut.

"No, Amy." I tried to lead her away. "Mommy's working."

Amy hung on to the doorknob. "I want Mommy," she insisted.

"How about a snack?" I tried.

"No! Mommy!" yelled Amy.

With increasing desperation, I suggested coloring books, modeling clay, a piggyback ride. But nothing worked.

"No, no, no," Amy screamed. "I want Mommy!" She

clung to the doorknob and started to kick the door. I pulled her loose and tried to carry her away, but she wriggled in my arms, kicking and shrieking so that finally I had to let go. She fell hard onto the floor, screaming. Behind me, the porch door banged open.

"What's the matter with you two, anyway? How am I supposed to get anything done?" Aunt Kate pushed her hair angrily off her face, leaving a smear of yellow paint across her bangs, as she crossed the room to pick Amy up. "Honestly, Alice, couldn't you have kept her busy a little longer?"

"No," I snapped back, as angry as she was. "I tried, but she's being just awful. Nobody could keep her busy."

For a long moment, Aunt Kate stood staring fiercely at me, her blue eyes cold, while Amy snuffled sulkily against her shoulder. Defiant, I stared back.

Then the fierceness abruptly went out of Aunt Kate's face. She sighed, smiled, and reached out to pat my shoulder. "I'm sorry, sweetie," she said. "I know how difficult Amy can be. I guess I just hate to be interrupted. I got much too grumpy."

"Well, I'm sorry, too, Aunt Kate," I said, though I still felt a little angry. "I really did try to keep her busy."

"I know you did. It's okay. Anyway, the rain's supposed to stop later. Maybe, if it does, you could take her outside for a while, and I could try again." Aunt Kate looked down into Amy's red, tear-smeared face. "Now, what are we going to do with you, pumpkin? How about if I read you a story?"

"Okay!" Amy broke into a smile, and they settled down on the couch with a stack of books.

Instead of sitting down beside them with my own book,

I found myself roaming away, into the kitchen and out the door onto the porch, where the rain drummed on the roof and streamed over the eaves in sheets, making the porch into a room with walls of rain. I dropped into Grandpa's rocker and stared resentfully out at the downpour.

The rain would be soaking my hideout, running freely through the pine-branch roof, streaming down the insides of the log walls, soaking the seats, making the dirt floor into mud. It was a good thing I hadn't left my sketchbook or Amy's books there. Even if the rain did stop later, the hideout would be so wet that I wouldn't be able to sit in there to draw that day.

It was only one day, I tried to tell myself, and the hideout would dry out quickly when the sun came out, so I could go back tomorrow. I was lucky, I reminded myself, that we'd had so little rain that summer. But I didn't feel lucky. I felt as sulky and resentful as Amy, kicking furiously at the door when Aunt Kate wouldn't come out. I didn't want to miss a day of drawing, and I felt a bit like having a tantrum myself.

I got up and stomped back into the kitchen, leaving Grandpa's rocker thumping noisily against the floorboards behind me as I slammed the door.

Aunt Kate's voice rose and fell musically in the living room, punctuated by Amy's occasional giggles. They sounded so cheerful that I couldn't stand to go in there. I was tired of Amy, tired of Aunt Kate, tired of the cabin. I wanted to get off by myself, or to see Grandpa, or one of my friends, or even Joe. I wanted to be at the hideout, at Grandpa's house, at home—anywhere, in fact, but where I was. I wanted something so badly that I felt almost hungry, but I didn't know what it was.

When my eyes fell on the canister of oatmeal on top of the refrigerator, I decided to make cookies, even though I knew food wasn't what I was hungry for. At least cooking would keep me busy. The stainless steel mixing bowl made a satisfying clatter when I yanked it out of the cabinet. I dumped oats and raisins and sugar and butter into the bowl and mixed it up by hand, pummeling the batter furiously with my wooden spoon.

Making the cookies took up the rest of the morning, and by the time the first batch was done, some of my bad temper had eased. When Aunt Kate and Amy appeared in the kitchen, drawn by the homey aroma of the cookies cooling on the counter, I managed to smile at them both.

We had a cheerful, backward lunch—cookies first, soup and sandwiches after—while the rain went on falling steadily outdoors. After Aunt Kate and I had cleared away the dishes and cleaned up the cookie sheets, we went back into the living room, where Amy was so quietly busy with a puzzle that it seemed as if some other child must have thrown the morning's tantrum.

The coffee table was heaped with Amy's picture books. On top of the stack lay a small book with a cover made of pine boards, held together with leather thongs. I gasped and pounced on it.

"The guest book! I forgot all about this! Where was it, Aunt Kate?"

"It was in the bookcase, under the pile of picture books. I was glad to see it, too." Aunt Kate smiled down at the book in my hands.

I opened its wooden cover carefully. The entry on the first page, in Grandma's delicate, old-fashioned handwriting, read, "Opened cabin today for the summer. Saw two sparrow hawks and a horned lark. Ruth and Katie played in the sandpile all day long."

Ruth and Katie; that was my mother and Aunt Kate, so young then that they still played in the sandpile. The guest book was a kind of cabin journal; it had been kept in the bookcase by the window ever since Grandpa built the place, and we always wrote a sentence or two in it when we came for a visit. By now the entries had been accumulating for so many years that Grandpa had had to add extra pages to the back of the book.

I flipped through the first pages, which I had read hundreds of times. Grandma had written almost all the early entries, and most of them were short and practical. "Put in new screens on back porch this weekend," read one entry, and "Shut off water for winter today," read another.

But here and there Grandpa had written a longer one, in his black, sprawling writing. I read one of these out loud. " 'Katie climbed up onto the roof this afternoon and scared us all out of a year's growth. She was all ready to jump off when I came out and stopped her—said she wanted to learn to fly.' "

I glanced up at Aunt Kate. "Did you really do that?"

"Oh, yes." Aunt Kate grinned ruefully down at the page. "I remember that day very well. I was sure I could fly, Alice, if I could just figure out how. I had been trying all day to do it by jumping off the porch steps, and I thought if I could just get a little more height, I could stay up. So I shinnied up the porch post and got ready to jump off the roof. I was so mad at Ruthie when she ran inside and got Dad. I thought she was an awful tattletale."

"Was she really a tattletale?" I asked, both pleased and

horrified. This was my mother Aunt Kate was talking about, after all, the mother who was always telling me not to be a tattletale when I told on Joe.

"No, she wasn't, not really," said Aunt Kate. "She was just trying to take care of me. The trouble was, I didn't want her to."

I understood that perfectly. Joe had always thought he was supposed to take care of me, whether I liked it or not.

On the next page was another of Grandpa's entries, dated the same summer. "Ruthie learned to ride her bike without training wheels today—rode up and down the lane all afternoon, pleased as punch. Katie climbed on the bike when we weren't looking, fell off, and cut her knee. Needed three stitches."

"You sure got into a lot of trouble, Aunt Kate," I said.

Aunt Kate shook her head. "It did seem that way. That day with Ruthie's bike, I was jealous that she could ride and I couldn't. But when I tried, the bike was just too big. I couldn't even reach the pedals. It was awful—one more thing Ruthie was good at, but I just couldn't do. She was always good at things, and I never was."

"But Aunt Kate," I objected. "I don't understand. You're good at a lot of things. You turned out to be the artist."

"Yes, but I didn't know that then," said Aunt Kate. "Sometimes it takes a while to find out what you're good at. Your mother was older than me, and I thought then that I would never catch up with her. Sometimes I still think I won't."

I was confused. "But she's just a mother. And a teacher, too, of course, but that's not a talent."

"Oh, yes it is. To be a good one takes a lot of talent, and your mother's a good teacher. And it's hard to be a good mother, too, you know. Ruthie must be a very good mother, and your father a very good father, to raise kids like you and Joe. You're a lot like your mother in that way, Alice. You're good at so many things."

Startled, I glanced up. "But I'm not, Aunt Kate. Not like Joe, anyway."

"Oh, come on, Alice. You have lots of talents."

"Like what?" I didn't mean to fish for compliments. I really wanted to know.

"Well, cooking, for instance. You certainly have a talent there. Those cookies you made this morning were terrific. And your blueberry pie would sell for five dollars a slice in New York City."

"It would?" A smile was beginning to tug at the corners of my mouth. I had never thought of cooking as a talent— it was just something I liked to do.

"Yes, it would," said Aunt Kate firmly. "And I happen to know you're good at art, too. Otherwise, you wouldn't be winning art contests."

I felt my smile vanish as quickly as it had appeared. There was that stupid art contest again. I wished I could go back to the beginning of the summer, like rewinding a videotape, and erase the part of our conversation when I'd made up winning that contest.

I looked away from Aunt Kate and flipped quickly through the guest book. On one page, near the end, was a picture I had drawn in the book when I was five or six, an awkward scrawl in crayon of a princess in a dress of many colors, with a tall crown and hair that reached the floor. Embarrassed, I turned past it quickly.

A few pages later I found an entry in my mother's grown-up writing, round and clear and firm.

"Kate and Tony's wedding today—reception here, out on the lawn. Wonderful party. Alice thrilled to be the flower girl, Tony dashing, Katie splendid in white Mexican cotton. Everyone danced all afternoon."

I tried to turn the page, thinking it might hurt Aunt Kate's feelings to remember her wedding. But she stuck her finger into the book to stop me.

"We did have fun that day," she said, not sounding sad at all. "I was head over heels in love."

"Aunt Kate," I asked cautiously, "what happened? I mean, if you were in love, why did you and Uncle Tony split up?"

Aunt Kate didn't say anything for a minute. When she spoke again, she did sound sad. "I don't know, exactly, Alice. I think we were just too young to get married. I was, anyway. Too young to know what I really wanted."

We sat quietly for a moment, listening to Amy singing one of her nonsense songs to herself as she finished her puzzle. There was something different about the silence, and after a moment, I realized what it was. The rain had finally stopped.

Aunt Kate noticed it, too, and she stood up and stretched. "What do you think about taking our little friend here outside now for a while?" she said. "She could splash around in the puddles, and maybe I could get a little work done before it's time to think about supper."

"Okay," I said, though I didn't really want our conversation to end. I closed the guest book carefully and set it on the top shelf of the bookcase, safely out of Amy's reach.

Amy didn't object, this time, when Aunt Kate went off onto the sun porch to paint. When I suggested a walk, she happily pulled her red rubber boots onto the wrong feet and ran ahead of me out the door.

Outdoors, though the rain had stopped, the sun still hid behind the clouds. Thunder rumbled grumpily in the distance, as if another storm was on the way. Everything was drenched. So much water was dripping down through the leaves that under the trees it sounded as if it were still raining. We obviously couldn't go into the woods, so instead we ran through the wet grass to the lane, where Amy jumped in the puddles and laughed when the brown water splattered her legs.

I worked my feet out of my sneakers and, barefoot, waded after Amy into a puddle. The water was cool, and I had forgotten how good it felt to wiggle my toes in soft, squishy mud. I was standing there happily exploring the muddy bottom of the puddle with my toes when I heard footsteps, slow and uncertain, splashing toward us around the curve in the lane, from the direction of the Bird House.

Something, I don't know what, made me grab Amy and duck into a clump of bushes. I crouched among the wet leaves, one arm around Amy and a finger on her lips. Surprisingly enough, Amy seemed to understand that we were hiding. She kept quiet beside me, and I peered through the dripping leaves and saw Madame Merlina appear on the road, using a furled black umbrella as a cane.

She stopped a few steps away from us and squinted down the road toward the cabin, as if she was looking for something. Then she sighed and turned around, walking back slowly toward the Bird House, splashing through the puddles as if she didn't see them.

I kept Amy in the bushes as long as she was willing to keep quiet, and then hurried back to the cabin with her, where we played on the front porch until it was time to go inside for dinner. I had an uncomfortable suspicion that Madame Merlina had been looking for me.

11

The next morning, I got out of bed into stale, heavy air, so hot I didn't want to get dressed. Instead of being cool and fresh, the way weather usually is after a rain, the day was hot and sticky. Amy whined all the way through breakfast, and Aunt Kate was grumpy, too. She'd told me, the night before, that she hadn't gotten much painting done while Amy and I were outside. She'd started a new painting, of Camelot, the court of King Arthur and Queen Guinevere, and I guess it wasn't working out the way she wanted it to.

We were all hot and bad-tempered. Aunt Kate snapped at Amy when she spilled her Cheerios. Then, when I tried to help by taking the bunny to wipe it off, Amy started to whine.

"No, Alice, give it back. Give me back my bunny!"

"For heaven's sake, Alice," exclaimed Aunt Kate. "Give her back the bunny. Don't make her have another tantrum. I'll never get any work done!" She got up, marched across the room into the sun porch, and slammed the door behind her.

Amy cried harder then, and she kept on whining while, muttering under my breath, I got my drawing pad out, found Amy's sneakers under her crib, and put them on her so that we could finally get back to the hideout.

Though the sun was already blazing, the air was heavy

and still, and a bank of dark clouds lay in the northwestern sky. Even in the shade, it wasn't any cooler in the woods. All the way down the trail, Amy hung back, whimpering, so that I had to pull her along. I was sweaty by the time we finally made it to the hideout.

All the work to get there hardly seemed worth it. The air was muggy, and the hideout itself was still sodden from the rain. Water dripped from the pine branches when the top of my head brushed them, and the floor was more mud than dirt. The hideout smelled swampy, and the log chairs were still too wet to sit on. Gnats whined, just like Amy, in an irritating cloud around my head, and deerflies nipped at the back of my neck.

For the first time, the hideout seemed too small to me. Amy's whining and the heat seemed to fill it up and push me out. What I really wanted to do was forget about the hideout for that day. I wanted to take Amy up to the blackbird pond. There'd be a breeze at the pond. There always was, blowing over the hilltop across the open hay field. And the water would be so cool, silky cool, fresh and sparkling, with the red-winged blackbirds wheeling overhead. I hadn't been swimming since I got to the cabin. I could imagine just how that wonderful clear water would feel on my skin.

But we couldn't go. I couldn't get to the pond without walking past the Bird House. And if I did that, Madame Merlina might see me. She was looking for me, I knew. Even if we snuck around through the woods to get to the pond, she or Miss Abby might spot us, as exposed on the banks of the pond as minnows washed up on a beach.

And if Madame Merlina found me, she'd make me do the Ouija board with her again. It made me feel trapped.

I missed the pond and my dreaming rock, where I'd spent so many hot summer mornings in other years. It seemed as if Madame Merlina had taken the pond away from me, or as if I'd given it to her somehow, without meaning to, during those sessions with the Ouija board.

If only Madame Merlina wasn't such a nut, I thought resentfully. If only she hadn't dragged out that stupid Ouija board, I never would have made up all that foolishness about Atlantis. If only she hadn't believed it all. That was the worst part. Why couldn't she have had more sense, like a regular grown-up? Enough sense to know I was making it up—enough sense to stop me, before I got so far into trouble that I couldn't stop myself? It was all her fault.

Then a deerfly bit Amy, and she started to wail again. "Mommy! I want my mommy!"

"Okay, okay, we're going," I snarled, and dragged her by the arm out of the hideout and back through the birch trees. Amy tripped and fell, scraping her knee. Now she was crying too hard to walk. I picked her up remorsefully and carried her all the way back to the cabin, sweating under her weight, wiping her tears and her runny nose on my T-shirt. This is all Madame Merlina's fault, I thought again as I lugged Amy into the yard. If it weren't for her, we could be swimming.

The cabin was quiet and the sun porch door was still closed. I got Amy some juice and a cookie and brought them out onto the hot front porch. As she ate, her crying changed to sniffling, and gradually stopped altogether. Finally she put down her cup and scrambled, cheerful again, down the steps to the damp sandpile under the beech tree. I ducked inside to slip my sketchbook back into its hiding place. Then I picked up a book and went back outside to sit on the porch steps, where I could keep an eye on Amy while I read.

I was reading the Narnia books, by C. S. Lewis. I'd read them before, but they were the kind of books you could read over and over again and never get tired of. In the one I was reading, a girl named Lucy hid in an old wardrobe that turned out to be a magical doorway to another world, where Lucy and her brothers and sister became kings and queens. It was winter in the book, endless winter, cold, snowy, icy. Just reading about it, there in the hot sun on the porch steps, cooled me off a little.

If my life were like the Narnia books, I thought, the hideout would be a magic gate to some secret world, like Narnia, or Middle-earth, or Oz. Or Atlantis. What would it be like to become the queen of some magic land, the way Lucy had, I wondered—to discover, all of a sudden, that I really *was* a princess of lost Atlantis? I imagined riding through the streets in my royal carriage, listening to the crowds cheering for me, calling out my name—"Alice, Alice, Alice!"

It took me a moment to realize that I really was hearing my name.

"Alice? Alice!"

I looked up, blinking. Someone was standing over me, a dark silhouette in the bright midmorning sun. It took me a moment to recognize Madame Merlina, but when I did, I jumped up. She had sunglasses on, and they gave her a racy, mysterious air, like a movie star or a millionaire. But from the neck down, she was the usual Madame Merlina, all in black, leaning on a cane. I saw with dismay that she had the Ouija board tucked under her arm. She looked

104

as out of place in the everyday sunshine of the yard as if she were a wicked witch from my daydream, blown out of Oz by a storm.

"Well, say good morning, like a well-brought-up child," ordered Madame Merlina, taking off the sunglasses. "If in fact you are a well-brought-up child." Her words were severe, but she looked oddly uncertain, blinking as if the sunlight hurt her pale eyes, and her shoulders were hunched up nervously. Was she always like that, and I'd just never noticed before? Or was she worried about something? Maybe she felt as out of place as she looked.

For a moment, I forgot I was angry at her. I almost felt sorry for her. "Hi, Madame Merlina," I said, in the friendliest voice I could come up with. "I didn't expect you to drop in."

"Well, I have expected you," she said. "You haven't appeared in weeks. Where have you been?" Her voice was shaky.

"I wanted to come over," I said, not quite truthfully. "But we've been—um, we've been very busy." I sighed. Another lie. At least this one was for a good reason.

"Hmph. You have plenty of time for reading, I notice." Now she sounded more like her old self. I put my book down grumpily, not feeling so sorry for her anymore.

But Madame Merlina was still talking.

"I have come to meet your aunt," she announced. "Is she at home this morning?"

"My aunt?" I stammered. "You mean Aunt Kate?"

"Well, who else, child?" demanded Madame Merlina. "I don't know what has happened to manners today. We are neighbors, after all. We should be introduced. And it is time I discussed your spiritual abilities with her. Is she indoors?" She tried to step past me to the kitchen door.

"No, wait!" I jumped into her path. "You can't go in. At least, not right now. Um, Aunt Kate's painting. She doesn't like to be interrupted when she's working."

Well, that was true, at least, I told myself.

Madame Merlina thumped her cane on the porch steps in irritation. "Nonsense," she said. "As if painting pictures had anything to do with work." She turned away from the door, but she didn't go back down the porch steps. Instead, she sat down firmly in Grandpa's porch rocker, looking as if she planned to stay all day.

I stood by the door, my thoughts spinning as uselessly as a hamster wheel. The very idea of Madame Merlina discussing my "spiritual abilities" with Aunt Kate made me shiver. If Aunt Kate knew I had fooled an old lady this way, it would be much worse than that silly little lie about the art contest. She could get so mad sometimes, and she was already in a terrible mood. I didn't want her angry with me. And she would tell Grandpa, and he'd tell my parents. I had to get out of this mess somehow.

But there Madame Merlina sat, rocking firmly, her back straight, the Ouija board in her lap. What was I going to do?

Under the beech tree, Amy sang softly to herself while she buried her bunny in the sand. She didn't seem to notice that Madame Merlina was there. It was about eleven o'clock; I had an hour or two, probably, before Aunt Kate stopped work for lunch. If I could just get Madame Merlina to go back home, and take that Ouija board with her. . . .

But now Madame Merlina was removing the citronella candle from the porch table and setting out the Ouija board in its place. I glanced nervously in through the kitchen window. The room was dim and silent. For the moment, at least, Aunt Kate was safely in her studio at the back of the house.

"Come, Alice," directed Madame Merlina. "We will call up the princess again."

"Not on the porch!" I exclaimed. "We can't do that here!"

"Why on earth not?"

"Well," I stammered weakly, "I'm supposed to be watching Amy right now."

"Nonsense," Madame Merlina retorted. "We can see the child perfectly well from here. Sit down, Alice. We have already put this off too long."

I stood there helplessly for a moment, but I couldn't think of any more objections. I sighed, flopped down in the other rocker, and put my hands on the planchette.

"Close your eyes," ordered Madame Merlina. "Concentrate." But her instructions were unnecessary. My eyes were screwed tightly shut, and I was concentrating, though not on calling up a spirit. I was trying to think of a way out of the fix I was in. If only Aunt Kate didn't pick today to stop painting early!

"Owla," intoned Madame Merlina. "Princess Owla. Greetings! Are you there?"

I just sat there, letting my fingers lie still on the planchette. I should never have started this whole thing, I thought miserably. But maybe it wasn't too late just to stop. Maybe if I quit making up more stories, and never moved the planchette again, Madame Merlina would give up and forget about it. That's it, I decided. I would just sit there and do nothing, and maybe she would think the Princess Owla had gone away.

"Princess Owla, we seek you! Greetings! May we speak with you?" Madame Merlina asked again.

Nothing happened. Our hands lay there, my scratched brown fingers with their dirty nails across from Madame Merlina's pale, knobby, wrinkled ones. If the Ouija board were real, I thought, if spirits were real, something would answer Madame Merlina's question, and the planchette would move by itself, the way it had the first time I'd tried it, when it said I had been an owl in a past life.

Why had that happened, anyway? I hadn't pushed it, and I didn't really think Madame Merlina had, either, not now that I saw how seriously she took this whole business of spiritualism. What had, then?

Whatever had moved it that day, nothing did this time. Madame Merlina repeated her question a few more times, but it hung unanswered in the air. I didn't move; neither did Madame Merlina. The summer air was still and quiet; only Amy's soft singing in the sandpile disturbed the silence.

"Hmph," said Madame Merlina at last. "Perhaps we have waited too long and lost contact. We will have to attempt it again at another time." She took her fingers off the planchette, and I sighed in relief. But before the sigh was all the way out, Madame Merlina stood up, pushing back her chair.

"And now," she said, "your aunt will not object to a brief interruption from a neighbor, I am sure. I will go inside and find her."

"Wait!" I gasped. "Don't go! Let me—um—let me ask the questions. Maybe Princess Owla needs to hear from me." I glanced up at her frantically and saw, with great relief, that she was easing herself stiffly back down into the chair.

"I doubt that," she said. "Princess Owla's spirit has always responded to me before. But it is true that you are an unusually sensitive child. Ask your questions, then." She put her fingers back on the planchette and looked up at me with those pale eyes, one bushy brow lifted.

I took a deep breath. I had to come up with something, anything, to keep Madame Merlina from talking to Aunt Kate.

"Princess Owla, where are you? Are you there?" I asked, hoping I didn't sound as silly as I felt. Then I began to push the planchette quickly from letter to letter.

"I-N-T-E-R-F-E-R-E-N-C-E." As I read the letters I was spelling, I glanced nervously into the kitchen through the window beside me, but all I saw was the reflection of my own worried face. *"C-A-N-N-O-T G-E-T T-H-R-O-U-G-H."*

Madame Merlina gave a small gasp when the planchette began to move, and frowned intently as I slowly spelled out each word. As I let the planchette slide to a stop, she rapped her fingers on it.

"Is this the Princess Owla?" she demanded, sounding as irritated as if she'd gotten a wrong number on the phone.

I pushed the planchette to *yes*, feeling nervous about that suspicious look on Madame Merlina's face. What if she could see my fingers moving? I didn't know how bad her vision really was. She had walked all the way here, after all. And there was more light on this porch than there was in that dark alcove at the Bird House where she usually kept the Ouija board.

"Why are you unable to speak to us? What is the problem? I do not understand." Madame Merlina sounded as annoyed as if the Princess Owla were right there on the porch, being rude. I knew I had to come up with something quickly.

"S-T-A-T-I-C," I spelled wildly, before I could think of a better word. They probably didn't even know about static in Atlantis, for Pete's sake. Radios hadn't been invented yet. But Madame Merlina was nodding.

"I see, I see," she said. "We must be in an unfavorable place here. The aura is wrong. Maybe because your aunt is a creative person . . . maybe her aura is too strong."

I was so relieved to hear a reason that sounded spiritualistic that it was all I could do to stop myself from spelling out, R-I-G-H-T!

Madame Merlina kept talking. "Your highness," she said, "May we contact you again from my home, where we have conversed before?"

I paused, dismayed. I didn't want to commit myself to yet another session on the Ouija board. I needed to get this thing over with, not keep it going forever. But there didn't seem to be anything else to do. I pushed the planchette reluctantly across the board to Yes and then I made it spell F-A-R-E-W-E-L-L. If I couldn't end the whole foolish pretense, at least I could get this session over with. I took my fingers off the planchette quickly and stood up.

Then I had to think fast to get Madame Merlina off the porch and away from the cabin. She tried one more time to go inside and introduce herself to Aunt Kate. But I said everything I could think of to talk her out of it. I told her about a pressing deadline for Aunt Kate's paintings and the creative person's absolute need for privacy, and I promised to bring Aunt Kate to the Bird House soon for a visit, and I don't even know what else I said. I'm not sure I had ever made up so much complete nonsense in one morning before.

It worked, though. I finally persuaded Madame Merlina to go back home, but not before I'd promised to meet her at the Bird House for another Ouija board session later that day.

As she finally disappeared around the bend in the lane, I stood staring after her. It seemed to me that my tongue hurt from all the lying I had been doing. I didn't like the way Madame Merlina looked from behind, when I couldn't see her bristly eyebrows and her pale, compelling eyes. From the rear, picking her way cautiously along the rocky lane, she looked small and breakable, somehow, as if a strong wind would blow her over. I was relieved when she vanished at last behind a pine tree at the spot where the lane curved toward her house, and I didn't have to look at her anymore.

12

While Amy went on playing in the sand, I sat limply in the porch rocker for a while, recovering. It was almost lunchtime now, and I expected Aunt Kate to appear on the porch soon. But it wasn't Aunt Kate who showed up next. After a few minutes, I heard the rumble of a car engine not far off, and a moment later Grandpa's little blue car crunched its way around the curve and came to a stop beside Aunt Kate's beat-up red Volkswagen.

"Salutations!" Grandpa popped out of the car like a leprechaun.

"Grandpa!" Amy flew out of the sandpile and jumped into his arms. I ran, too, and Grandpa hugged us both at once.

"Came up to stay for the weekend," he said. "I talked it over with Katie on the phone this morning, and we thought this was a good time for a visit."

"That's great, Grandpa," I said, as I reached into the backseat for the old black leather doctor bag that Grandpa used for an overnight case.

But then, as Grandpa headed for the cabin with Amy in his arms, he called back to me over his shoulder, "Hey, I just had a chat with one of our neighbors. Met her on the road. Says she's a friend of yours, Alice Anne. You never told me you'd met Merlina Bird."

I straightened up so fast that I banged my head on the

car door frame. As the cabin door shut behind Grandpa and Amy, I dropped his bag in the grass and stood there rubbing the swelling on my head. Tears stung my eyes, but I wasn't sure whether they were from the bump or from the shock of what Grandpa had said.

What had Madame Merlina told him? Maybe she'd told him all about the princess Owla of Atlantis. Maybe she'd told him about my "spiritual abilities," the way she'd wanted to tell Aunt Kate. Maybe at that very minute Grandpa was thinking about what an awful liar I was.

In my whole life, I'd never hidden anything from Grandpa, or exaggerated anything, or lied about anything. I had never wanted to. But this summer everything had changed. Now I had a secret I had to keep from him, and I might have to lie to him, too, whether I wanted to or not—if it wasn't already too late. I couldn't let him find out about Princess Owla and the Ouija board.

It wasn't that I thought he'd yell at me. My father yelled, sometimes, but not Grandpa. I remembered once Joe and I were with Grandpa when he locked his keys in the car. Joe got very quiet and I held my breath, waiting for Grandpa to lose his temper the way Dad would have. But Grandpa just stared through the closed car window at the keys dangling in the ignition and scratched his head. Then he turned to us and shrugged. "Well, children," he said in his ordinary, gentle voice. "We seem to be in a predicament. What do you suggest?"

So I wasn't afraid he'd be angry, exactly. I guess it was because I knew he wouldn't be proud. And more than anything else in the world, I wanted Grandpa to be proud of me. So I stood there in the driveway, drawing circles in the sand with my toe, putting off as long as I could the moment when I would have to go inside and look him in the eye and find out what he knew about me.

Finally Aunt Kate stuck her head out the kitchen door and called, "It's almost lunchtime, Alice. Aren't you ever coming in?" and I couldn't avoid going indoors any longer.

I slunk into the kitchen, sure that the worry hanging over me showed as clearly as a cloud of dust. But nobody paid much attention to me. Grandpa was on the couch with Amy, bouncing her on his knees while she squealed in delight, and Aunt Kate was sitting on the floor sketching them, while a panful of grilled cheese sandwiches on the stove were burning black.

I grabbed the pan off the burner, threw out the charred sandwiches, and made some new ones, grateful for a reason to seem too busy to talk. It would have been too hard to talk, anyway, around the lump of anxiety in my throat.

When we sat down for lunch, I couldn't eat. All I could think about was whether Grandpa knew about me and Madame Merlina. He seemed perfectly normal; he teased me just the way he always did, and his face when he looked at me wore his own familiar, loving expression. Maybe he didn't know, after all. But I didn't feel relieved. I nibbled a little at the edges of my sandwich and finally hid it in my napkin and just sat there, trying not to meet Grandpa's eyes and hoping nobody would notice how quiet I was.

But Grandpa was a doctor, and it was his job to notice things like that. When I jumped up after lunch to carry the plates into the kitchen, hoping to dump my uneaten sandwich into the trash before anybody noticed it, he looked up sharply, followed me into the kitchen, and caught me just as the sandwich tumbled into the can.

"Didn't eat, eh? Feeling sick?" He laid a hand on my

forehead. It felt wonderful there, cool and comforting, and I pushed my head against it, feeling a little like a dog asking to be petted.

"No fever, I guess," he said, frowning down at me. "But you're pale, all right, and I didn't know you could be so quiet. Something wrong, Alice Anne?"

Standing there by the garbage can, feeling as awful as if I really were sick, I almost opened my mouth and told him the whole story. I could feel the words crowding onto my tongue like a mob of prisoners fighting to get out, and I wanted, badly, to stop holding them in. But Grandpa's eyes shone down at me through his glasses, full of love and pride and concern, and I thought how disappointed those eyes would be if he knew how I had lied. I couldn't stand the thought. I closed my mouth on all those words, trapping them behind my teeth, and I shook my head at Grandpa.

"Nothing," I said, tasting the bitterness of the first direct lie I'd ever told my grandfather. "Nothing's wrong. My stomach's a little upset, that's all."

"Hmm." Grandpa just stood there studying me for a second. Then, abruptly, he turned away, and I felt released, as if his eyes had been a magnet holding me in place.

Grandpa grabbed his beat-up fishing hat off a hook and clapped it onto his bald head. "What about a walk?" he said. "Think those blueberries ought to be getting ripe. Come help me pick some?"

"Well, okay." I picked up two berry cans and followed him down the porch steps and across the hot yard, feeling a little better. Surely, if Grandpa knew anything about me and Madame Merlina, he'd have said so by now.

We didn't talk as we waded through the Indian paintbrush and Queen Anne's lace growing knee-deep in the unmown yard, nor as we pushed our way through the pine trees to where the wild blueberry bushes covered the ground beyond the pines, their narrow leaves dusty green in the heat. Ripe berries glinted here and there, as blue as scattered bits of trapped summer sky.

"They're ripe, all right. Thought so," was all Grandpa said. I handed him a berry can and, wordlessly, we both crouched in the low bushes and began to pick.

Grandpa was a fast blueberry picker. I was a bit slower, because every other berry found its way into my mouth instead of my can. But there were so many berries hidden under the leaves that my can filled up quickly.

Everything at the berry patch was just the way it had always been, the tingly scent of crushed wintergreen under our feet, the fat, dusty feel of the berries as my fingers found them among the stiff leaves, their warm, purply sweetness in my mouth. But it didn't feel the same.

Other summers at the cabin, Grandpa and my mom would pick berries together, and sometimes while they picked they liked to quote poetry to each other. My mom knew yards of poetry, even more than Grandpa. There was one poem she'd recite sometimes that always sounded just like the berry patch to me.

" 'The lark's on the wing;/The snail's on the thorn:/ God's in his heaven,/All's right with the world!' " my mother would say, flourishing a berry and popping it into her mouth. "Robert Browning, 'Pippa Passes.' "

Usually, squatting in the berry patch with the sun on my shoulders, my can full of berries, and my mouth full of their warm summer sweetness, I knew just how Robert Browning must have felt when he wrote that. But this time I didn't feel that way. I had a crick in my neck from crouching, and the sun on my back was hot, not pleasantly warm. Even the berries didn't seem to taste right. All isn't right with the world, that's the trouble, I thought. Not with my world, anyway.

Grandpa's can was full. He stood up slowly, stretched, selected a single berry from his can, and ate it thoughtfully. Then he spoke.

"So this Merlina Bird tells me she's a spiritualist. Had a Ouija board under her arm, in fact. Know much about spiritualism, Alice Anne?"

I dropped my handful of berries. "Um—no," I said. "Not much." Was I lying? I didn't know much about spiritualism. But it felt like a lie anyway.

I glanced up at Grandpa. He was looking straight at me, his eyes friendly and curious, as blue as the berries behind his glasses. I looked away quickly and started to search among the bushes for the berries I'd dropped.

"Didn't know anybody did that stuff anymore," said Grandpa. "Used to be big around here, mediums and séances all over the place. All fakery, of course. Didn't think anyone still believed in all that."

"All fakery, Grandpa?" I didn't look up. "What do you mean?"

"Oh, there were a lot of charlatans in the spiritualist movement." Grandpa crouched back down and started picking berries into my can. "People faked all kinds of things. They had elaborate gadgets that made tables rap and pencils seem to write by themselves. There were plenty of fools ready to believe it all."

I turned my back on Grandpa and stood up, staring into the dark branches of the pine trees. As I watched, a blue jay landed on a branch. It opened its beak and squawked, a harsh, mocking sound, as if it were laughing at me.

But behind me, Grandpa kept picking berries and talking in his comfortable, rumbling voice. "Odd thing happened not far from here, in fact. Maybe a hundred years ago, two sisters, your age or thereabouts, learned how to crack the bones of their big toes inside their shoes. Made a loud noise, I guess, like a rifle shot, and they told their mother it was spirits rapping. She believed 'em, and before long they had people coming from far and wide to ask them questions. Ended up world famous, doing shows in the big cities, answering people's questions and telling fortunes, cracking their toes inside their boots all that time. Spiritualist leaders, they were."

"Is this a true story, Grandpa?" I asked suspiciously, not turning around to look at him.

"Sure," said Grandpa from behind me. "Wouldn't lie to you, would I?"

For a moment I couldn't say anything at all. The blue jay squawked again. Finally I managed to answer. "No, Grandpa," I said. "I guess you wouldn't. What—what happened to them?"

"Nothing happened," said Grandpa. "Nobody figured it out, and they just kept it up. They grew up, kept on cracking their toes and telling everyone it was messages from the spirit world. Did it all their lives. Then, when they got old, one of the sisters spilled the beans, told the newspapers how it was done, showed 'em how she could make her big toes rap without even moving her feet."

"Did she get in trouble?" I asked.

"Nope," said Grandpa. "By time that so many people believed in the fake spirits that when she told the truth, none of them believed her. People kept on coming to their shows and paying money to ask the spirits questions, and she and her sister kept on cracking their toes, and everybody more or less pretended together." Grandpa shook his head. "A funny business. Hope this friend of yours up here at the Bird House doesn't take it all too seriously."

I bent over to pick some berries and brought them up to my mouth, but I didn't eat them. All of a sudden blueberries seemed unappetizing, like eating a handful of stones. "All their lives?" I said. I could hear my voice cracking. "Those two girls spent their whole *lives* pretending?"

"Guess so," said Grandpa. "Kind of a sad story."

"It sure is." I threw my handful of berries at the blue jay, who flew off in a huff. The berries pattered down through the pine needles like raindrops. "But Grandpa," I said before I thought. "Once I used the Ouija board and it really did move. It answered a question. Nobody was faking it. What would make it do that?"

"Don't know," said Grandpa. "Some people say it's involuntary muscle movements. Or it could be real spirits."

"Grandpa!" I said.

"Well, why not?" asked Grandpa. "Who knows? Just because lots of spiritualists were fakers doesn't mean none of it's real. Just as unscientific to be certain there isn't a psychic world as to be sure there is one, seems to me. Think you and I are better off sticking with the real world, though." Grandpa straightened up and picked up my berry can. "Come on, Alice Anne, we've got enough berries here to last us awhile. Let's go see what Katie and Amy are up to."

"You go ahead, Grandpa," I said. "I think I'll take a walk."

Grandpa gave me one of his sharp looks. Then he dropped a light kiss on my head. "Don't get lost. See you soon."

I watched him disappear through the pine trees, a blueberry can dangling from each hand. But what I saw, in my mind's eye, was the two girls he'd told me about, cracking their big toes, pretending their lives away. I understood exactly what had happened to them, and I was afraid I knew just how they'd felt. Why had Grandpa told me that story, anyway? Maybe he did know about me and Madame Merlina, after all.

I could just go ask her, I thought. The idea arrived so suddenly that it startled me. Why hadn't I thought of it before? I could just go up to the Bird House and ask Madame Merlina what she had told Grandpa, right now. At least then I'd know.

"I'll just do it," I said to myself. "I'll go up there and ask her, right now."

13

I waited in the berry patch until I heard the bang of the screen door back at the cabin, telling me that Grandpa had gone inside. Then I pushed my way through the pine trees and ran, as fast as I could go, past the cabin and up the lane to the Bird House.

The place looked even crazier than I remembered, bright yellow in the midst of all those flamingos and ducks and flower beds. A brightly painted wooden windmill I hadn't seen before stood by the road, and the plastic owl I'd found for Miss Abby the last time I was there glared at me from the bed of petunias, almost as if it were accusing me of something.

Miss Abby was perched on a rickety ladder like a scoop of ice cream ready to fall off a cone, leaning way out to reach the top of a window frame she was painting. When she saw me, she waved her brush, scattering yellow drops on the grass.

"Hello, Alice! Like my paint job?"

I gulped as she leaned even further out to reach the far edge of the window. The ladder teetered. "It—it looks great, Miss Abby."

"Well, I think so myself," she puffed, straightening up to dip her brush into the bucket balanced on a rung of the ladder. "I can only do a little at a time, of course; I do get a bit tired. But it's so satisfying, Alice—almost as good as gardening. My sister says I can't do the second floor, that I'd better hire someone for the high spots. But I think I can do it, don't you?"

"Well, I don't know—" I began uncomfortably. But before I could think of a tactful way to say that I really thought she ought to stay off ladders altogether, the front door swung open and Madame Merlina appeared on the porch.

"You are here," she announced dramatically. "Come in, young Alice. I am ready to begin."

Until that moment I had completely forgotten that I had promised Madame Merlina I would come that afternoon to contact the Princess Owla. But clearly she remembered. I waved good-bye to Miss Abby, who flapped her brush cheerfully and called, "Have fun with your games, girls." Madame Merlina snorted in disgust, turned on her heel, and marched inside, and I followed, to find the candle burning in the alcove and the Ouija board all set out.

"Madame Merlina," I said, stopping in the middle of the living room. "Um—I wanted to ask you about something. Did you—did you meet my grandfather this morning?"

"I certainly did," she said, sitting down in one of the carved wooden chairs. "He is a very cordial gentleman. Please sit down, Alice. I am ready to begin."

I stood where I was, twisting my fingers together. "Um—well—I was wondering—what did you talk about?"

"That," said Madame Merlina firmly, "is not your affair. Sit down, child."

"But—" I said. "I'm sorry, Madame Merlina, but I

really need to know. Did you tell him about the Ouija board?"

"Child, you are wasting my time," said Madame Merlina impatiently.

"I am not!" Why was she always so bossy? "It's important, Madame Merlina. I really need to know! I—I won't contact the Princess Owla again until you tell me!"

I stopped, breathless, surprised by my own outburst. Madame Merlina raised her bristly eyebrows.

"You are being very rude, child," she said. "But if you must know, yes, we did discuss spirituality. He asked me about the Ouija board, since I was carrying it when we met."

"But what about me?" I begged. "Madame Merlina, did you tell him about me?"

"What about you?" Madame Merlina tapped her fingers irritably on the table.

"About the princess Owla!" I wailed. "Did you tell him that?"

She sighed. "If you are asking whether I told him about our contact with the princess Owla, I have not yet done so, although I would certainly like to. I did mention that you were interested in spiritualism, but I did not discuss your abilities. I am sure he will be fascinated to learn of them when we have another opportunity to converse. Now, will you please join me?"

I dropped into the other chair, my legs as limp as cooked spaghetti with relief. I felt like a prisoner whose pardon has arrived from the governor five minutes before the execution. I hardly noticed as Madame Merlina began her Ouija board ritual, placing her fingers on the planchette, ordering me to concentrate, closing her eyes to call for Princess Owla.

My mind was so full of relief that I didn't even try to think up an excuse not to do the Ouija board. When Madame Merlina intoned, "Princess Owla, are you able to communicate with us now?" I just pushed the planchette obediently to *Yes*. What difference did it make, anyway? How could doing it one more time make things any worse than they were already?

"Princess Owla, please tell us about Atlantis," directed Madame Merlina.

"What about it?" I asked in my ordinary voice, forgetting to move the planchette or to try to sound spiritual.

Madame Merlina glared at me. "Not you, Alice. I am addressing the princess Owla," she said severely.

"Of course." I looked guiltily back down at my hands. "Sorry."

Madame Merlina cleared her throat. "Princess Owla," she said formally. "Atlantis no longer exists in our world, and so we are curious about your country. We would like you to tell us about it. Please, what is Atlantis like?"

She waited expectantly, but I just sat there. What could I say about Atlantis? I didn't know anything about it, and just then I didn't think I could invent anything. After the scare about Grandpa, my brain felt all used up and empty.

"Hmm," said Madame Merlina after a moment, when the planchette didn't move. "Princess Owla, would you prefer me to ask specific questions?"

I pushed the planchette gratefully to the word *Yes*.

"That is the usual procedure, after all," said Madame Merlina agreeably. "Let me see . . . what are your foods? Tell us, what do you eat?"

It was odd that she asked about food just then, because my stomach was grumbling, and I was thinking regretfully about the lunch I had cooked but hadn't eaten: grilled muenster cheese on pumpernickel bread, my favorite.

"C-H-E-E-S-E," I spelled, reading the word wistfully. My mouth watered. "B-R-E-A-D. P-U-M-P-E-R-N-I-C-K-E-L B-R-E-A-D." It took a long time to push the planchette around all those letters, and I had to pause halfway through *pumpernickel* while I tried to remember how to spell it. But I could almost taste that sandwich.

"Pumpernickel?" Madame Merlina echoed me doubtfully. "You have pumpernickel bread in Atlantis? How unexpected. I thought pumpernickel bread was German."

Ouch, I thought. That was a mistake. I was going to have to concentrate harder.

"A-T-L-A-N-T-I-S I-N-V-E-N-T-E-D I-T F-I-R-S-T," I spelled quickly.

"I see," said Madame Merlina, sounding as if she didn't, quite. "Bread—cheese—is that all? Is your diet vegetarian, then?"

I knew that a vegetarian was a person who didn't eat meat, because Chloe and I went through a stage together once when we stopped eating meat because we started feeling sorry for animals. We got over it together, too, at a cookout at my house on the Fourth of July, when neither of us could resist the wonderful smell of my father's charcoal-broiled steak.

I pushed the planchette to *No*, and then made it spell "W-E E-A-T F-I-S-H."

"Ah." Madame Merlina looked happier. "What kinds of fish?"

"T-U-N-A," I spelled out quickly. It was the only kind

of fish I could think of. Then I paused, stuck for a minute. What other kinds of fish were there? Not trout. I knew from fishing trips with Grandpa that they lived in fresh water. I tried to remember what I'd seen on our class trip to the Boston Aquarium.

"*S-H-A-R-K-S. C-R-A-B-S. O-C-T-O-P-U-S-E-S.*" I spelled the last word quickly and read it out with a note of finality, hoping Madame Merlina wouldn't expect me to come up with any more.

"Octopuses?" asked Madame Merlina. The surprised look was back on her face. "What do you do with those?"

I didn't have any idea how people cooked octopuses. Maybe they were even poisonous. I wouldn't eat one, I was sure of that. "*S-O-U-P,*" I spelled, grasping at straws. "*O-C-T-O-P-U-S B-O-N-E S-O-U-P.*"

It was airless and hot in the dark parlor, and I was sweating. I wiggled in my chair, wishing I could get up and leave. Madame Merlina hadn't told Grandpa about me and the Ouija board, after all. I could have just gone off to the hideout and spent the afternoon drawing. I wished I had.

Madame Merlina frowned down at our four hands close together on the planchette. "What about architecture?" she asked. "What kind of building do you live in?"

I squirmed. Why was she asking such boring questions? It was fun to daydream about an imaginary world, about dancing princesses and magic. But this was no fun at all; it was like taking a social studies test. I sighed and made myself make the Ouija board spell something.

"*C-A-S-T-L-E.*" I dragged the planchette around the board. This spirit was supposed to be a princess, after all. A castle seemed like the right place for her to live.

"Ah." Madame Merlina sat up a little straighter. "Tell

me about it," she demanded. "What is it made of? How big is it?"

But I couldn't think of anything to say about the castle. I knew Madame Merlina was waiting for me, and I closed my eyes and tried to picture it—on a hilltop, maybe— what was it like?

Come on, Alice, I told myself, just come up with something, anything. But I couldn't. Another image floated in front of my eyes instead—my hideout, all by itself in the woods, real and simple and ordinary, and somehow, more special than any castle I could think of.

"Princess Owla?" asked Madame Merlina finally. "What is your castle built of?"

My fingers almost seemed to move by themselves. *"L-O-G-S,"* I spelled.

"Logs!" Madame Merlina blinked down at our hands. "A log castle? I have never heard of such a thing. Why do you call it a castle?"

"B-E-C-A-U-S-E I-T I-S M-I-N-E." I spoke the words almost faster than my fingers could push the planchette.

"Yours?" Madame Merlina was frowning now, looking a little confused. "I do not understand."

I sat still for a moment, thinking. How could I explain the magic of the hideout, one word at a time, in this slow, dragging, Ouija board way? I wanted to stop pushing the silly planchette and just tell Madame Merlina all about my hideout, about the green dappled light that came in through the pine roof, and the log furniture I'd found for it, and how nice the birds sounded in the trees. I wished I could tell her about how exciting it was to start learning to draw. But of course, I couldn't tell her any of those things.

All of a sudden I wished so fiercely to be in the hideout

that I could almost smell the pine branches on the roof and feel the rough log walls against my back. I wished I could teleport myself there, right out of Madame Merlina's stuffy old parlor, away from the Ouija board and the problems it had brought me, and away from everybody else, too. Away, most of all, from all this pretending.

"*I-T I-S M-Y S-E-C-R-E-T P-L-A-C-E.*" I said the words so fast that I got ahead of the Ouija board and had to shove the planchette, fast, around the letters until I caught up with myself. Then I went on spelling, more slowly, "*M-I-N-E. O-N-L-Y M-I-N-E.*"

"What do you do there?" asked Madame Merlina. There was an odd expression on her face. She seemed to have softened somehow. She was listening hard, and she looked suddenly younger. For a minute I thought, watching her face, that she would like the hideout, that safe, private world, just as much as I did.

"*N-O-T-H-I-N-G.*" I shoved the planchette almost angrily across the Ouija board. "*I A-M J-U-S-T M-E.*"

"Just you? I am sorry, I still do not understand," said Madame Merlina again. "Just the Princess Owla?"

"*N-O-T P-R-I-N-C-E-S-S,*" I spelled. "*J-U-S-T M-E.*"

"You don't like being a princess?" asked Madame Merlina wistfully.

"*N-O,*" I spelled. "*I H-A-T-E I-T.*" There was a lump starting to form in my throat, and I could feel tears burning my eyes. I tried to spell some more, but I couldn't push the planchette around to the letters fast enough to keep up with the rush of my words, so I just shoved it around in random circles as words erupted out of me. "It's not me. I'm not a princess. I'm just an ordinary person. It's awful to pretend to be what you're not." I forgot to try to sound like the Princess Owla, or any way except the way I really felt; I just let the words come out.

Madame Merlina lifted her fingers off the planchette and frowned at me, looking as if she was about to ask me something.

But before she could, I jumped to my feet.

"I have to go now," I said quickly, scrubbing at my eyes before tears could spill out, backing away from her. "I—um—I forgot something. I'll see you later. Bye!"

And before she had a chance to stop me or even to say good-bye, I ran out of the shadowy alcove and across Miss Abby's plant-filled living room. My eyes weren't used to the light, and besides, they were half blinded with tears. I collided with a geranium in a big clay pot, banging my shin, and as I hopped on the other foot, my funny bone cracked painfully against the door frame. Hugging my elbow, limping on my banged leg, I clattered across the porch and down the steps. I could hear Miss Abby's surprised voice calling to me as I ran past the foot of her ladder, but I just waved blindly in her direction, choked out something past the lump in my throat, and kept running, past that stupid plastic owl and out of the yard.

I felt as if I were running away from something chasing me. But no matter how fast I ran, all the way back to the cabin the ache went with me, in shin and funny bone and stinging eyes and burning throat, and, worst of all, in my heart.

14

As I ran into the yard, still swallowing down sobs, the kitchen door opened and Grandpa came out. I wasn't ready for him to see me. I knew I looked as upset as I felt. But it was too late to hide behind the beech tree; he was already waving at me as he came down the porch steps.

I wiped quickly at my eyes with the back of my hand, trying to calm down before he got close enough to see my face.

But instead of coming toward me, Grandpa went straight to his parked car. "Hi, Alice Anne," he called as he opened the door. "Sorry, but I have to run out on you. Just got a call from the hospital—patient of mine's having a baby earlier than I thought she would. Got to get down there."

"Oh, Grandpa, no," I protested. But I didn't mean it. What I felt was relief.

Grandpa was looking in my direction, but I could tell that he didn't really see me. His mind was already on his patient. My cheeks felt hot and red, and my eyes were still wet with the tears I hadn't let fall. But Grandpa didn't notice, and I was glad.

"I'll be back later tonight, I hope," he said, sliding into the car and checking his watch. "Tomorrow morning, anyway. Better run now. Bye, honey."

"Bye, Grandpa." I waved as his car pulled away, wheels spinning on the sandy road. It was the first time I could remember that I'd ever been glad to see Grandpa driving away.

I went through the rest of that day like a robot. I did all the right things—read some books to Amy, helped Aunt Kate cook dinner, gave Amy a bath—but all that time I felt almost numb, as if I weren't really there at all.

While Aunt Kate put Amy to bed, I did the dishes, drying every cup and spoon much more carefully than necessary. Then I tried to read, but the story didn't make sense. All I could think about was Madame Merlina and her stupid Ouija board, and how she had said she was looking forward to telling Grandpa about my spiritual abilities the next time she had a chance to talk to him.

The evening was no cooler than the day had been; it was hot and stuffy in the cabin, and no breezes blew through the open windows. I couldn't concentrate, and I couldn't sit still. I wandered restlessly around the cabin, picking up Chloe's latest letter and putting it down again, looking out the window, twiddling knobs on the radio.

After a while, Aunt Kate came out of Amy's room. She sat down in Grandpa's rocking chair with a pile of sketchbooks, put on a pair of reading glasses, and started going through some old drawings. I peered over her shoulder. She was looking at a sketch of a woman with no clothes on. The woman in the picture looked cold and uncomfortable, leaning on one arm, with her back twisted so that the bones of her spine jutted out strangely.

"I got that backbone all wrong," Aunt Kate muttered. She added a couple of quick lines to the back of the woman's neck, and the whole drawing was suddenly different, as if it had come to life. "You have to get the bones right, or the whole thing won't work."

"Aunt Kate, do octopuses have bones?" I asked suddenly.

"Octopuses? I'm not sure," said Aunt Kate. "I'm not sure this model had any bones, either, judging by the way I drew her. At least, not normal ones. Why did you want to know?"

I backed away. "Oh, I don't know," I said. "I was just wondering." I flopped down on the couch and stared at the ceiling.

"I don't think octopuses do have any bones," said Aunt Kate, frowning thoughtfully at me over the drawing. "They just have cartilage or something. Ask Grandpa when he gets back. It's the kind of thing he knows about." She flipped to a new drawing. "Hmm, this one's better."

"Great," I said. I bit moodily at a fingernail. I wondered whether Madame Merlina knew about octopus bones. She had looked a little taken aback by the octopus bone soup I'd said they made in Atlantis. "Just great," I said again.

This must be the way those two girls who cracked their toes felt, I thought bitterly. I bet if I met them, we'd get along fine. I'd like to try to call up one of their spirits on the Ouija board and ask their advice. But what good would that do? Their lies had gotten away from them even worse than mine had—at least I didn't have crowds of strangers showing up to stare at me. In the end they'd ruined their whole lives. And if Grandpa found out about me and the Ouija board, my life would be just about ruined, too. I let out a miserable sigh.

"Alice, what's the matter?" Aunt Kate looked up as she

turned a page. Her glasses slid down her freckled nose like a cartoon schoolteacher's, but even so she looked beautiful. "You've been unlike yourself all day. Do you feel okay?"

"I feel fine," I said hastily. I sat up and stretched my face into what I hoped was a cheerful smile. "I really do feel fine, Aunt Kate. I'm just a little—um—homesick, that's all."

"Homesick!" Aunt Kate put her sketchbook aside. "Of course you are. I keep forgetting you're only twelve and you've never been away from your parents before. It must get lonely for you here."

I wiggled uncomfortably on the couch. I wasn't homesick. It was getting so nothing I said was exactly true anymore. "Aunt Kate, I haven't been lonely. I've—I've been having a very exciting summer so far."

I waited unhappily for her to ask me just what was so exciting about watching a three-year-old every day all by myself. But at that moment the telephone rang, and Aunt Kate got up to answer it. I fled into the kitchen and got down a box of cookies, so glad for the interruption that at first I didn't listen to Aunt Kate's conversation. But as I came back into the living room with a handful of Oreos, I realized she was talking to Grandpa.

"Okay, we'll look for you in the morning, then, Dad," she was saying. "I hope your patient has a beautiful baby. Oh, Dad, I forgot to tell you before you left, we have a dinner invitation. Abigail Bird called while you and Alice were out this afternoon—you know, she's one of the ladies in that old house up the road—and asked all of us up there to eat tomorrow night. I said we'd be glad to come. You'll be back in time, right?"

I gazed at her in horror. Abigail Bird—that was Miss

Abby, of course. Dinner at the Bird House, with Madame Merlina and Aunt Kate and Grandpa all together in one room? "Oh, no," I said out loud, before I could stop myself. But Aunt Kate didn't hear me.

"Good," she was saying into the phone. "It should be interesting. They seem like an unusual pair, and I haven't really met either one of them yet. See you in the morning, then, Dad. But drive carefully, okay? And try not to stay up all night if you can help it. We love you. G'night."

Aunt Kate hung up the phone and turned to me. "I guess you heard that was Grandpa," she said. "The baby's taking its time getting born, so he won't be back till very late. Did you hear what I told him about going up to the neighbors' house tomorrow night?"

I nodded dumbly.

"Sorry I forgot to tell you before," said Aunt Kate. "Oh, good, cookies. I forgot about those, too. I forget everything these days. It's painting so much; it makes me absentminded. Anyway, I'm glad the Bird sisters invited us, aren't you? I feel terrible that I haven't been up there yet to say hello."

Aunt Kate went into the kitchen, and I could hear the Oreo package rustling, but I couldn't think of a thing to say. I stood in the middle of the living room, stunned. They'd find out; that was what was going to happen. Aunt Kate and Grandpa would find out about the way I'd been fooling Madame Merlina, and there was nothing I could do to stop it.

Lying there on the rocking chair was Aunt Kate's sketchbook. She'd left it open to the drawing she'd done of me that night earlier in the summer, when I had thought maybe she'd make me look like a princess. My own face, my own eyes stared up at me from the sketchbook, still looking stupidly hopeful. I slapped the sketchbook shut.

I didn't know what to do. If it had still been light outside, I would have gone to my hideout, just to be by myself so that I could think. But it was getting dark now, too dark to find my way through the woods. I did the next best thing—I went into my room, shut the door firmly, and went to bed, without even saying good-night to Aunt Kate.

I didn't sleep much that night. I tossed around in my bed, worrying, trying to come up with a plan that would make it impossible for us to go to the Bird House.

I could pretend to be sick, and then we'd have to stay home. But I'd always found it hard to fake illness. Grownups could tell by feeling my forehead whether I was feverish, so it didn't work to heat up the thermometer under hot water or something. And I could never remember to act sick for very long—I always forgot eventually and ate something, or burst out laughing at somebody's joke, and my mother would say, "Ha! A miraculous recovery!" and send me off to school. And besides, Grandpa was a doctor. He'd see through me in a minute. No, that would never work.

Maybe I could pretend that the sisters had called back to cancel their invitation. I could tell Grandpa and Aunt Kate that they had called while they were outside, or something. . . . But then what would happen the next time one of them talked to the Bird sisters? And anyway, the thought of all the lies I would have to tell to get away with that made me feel sick.

Maybe, I thought, I could fall out of the beech tree,

accidentally on purpose, and break my arm. It would hurt, of course, but it would make a great excuse, and everyone else would probably stay home with me. But with my luck, I thought, tugging at my twisted, sweaty sheets, I'd break my back instead and have to spend the rest of my life in a wheelchair.

No, falling out of the tree wouldn't work, either. But what would? I couldn't think of anything. But I had to think of something. I lay there listening to the wind rushing louder and louder through the trees. It sounded as if a storm was coming, and I wished that it would, to cool off the muggy air in my little room. But the storm didn't come, and I dozed fitfully, too hot and too worried to sleep.

Sometime during the night I heard Grandpa come in. I listened to him move around the cabin, getting himself something to eat in the kitchen, taking a shower, opening the squeaky fold-out couch in the living room. On any other night I probably would have gotten up to have some cocoa with him. But this time I stayed silently behind my closed door. Even after I heard his mattress creak as he lay down and the click of the living room light snapping off, I still lay awake in the dark, feeling lonelier than I could remember ever having felt before.

15

I watched the sky outside my window gradually lighten to a pearly silver as the sun got ready to rise. But before it did, I must finally have fallen deeply asleep, because the next thing I knew, it was morning, and Amy was sitting on my chest.

"Get up, Alice," she instructed me. "Morning time. Get up!"

I moaned in protest and squeezed my eyes shut. But Amy bounced on my stomach. "Come on," she insisted. "Get up now."

"Oh, all right, all right," I groaned. "But you have to get off me, Amy, so I can."

Amy hoped off obediently and I rolled out of bed, my bones aching as if I were Madame Merlina's age.

"Where is everybody?" I asked as I sleepily pulled on a pair of jeans and a sweatshirt. It had cooled off during the night. It was only the beginning of August, but the air was chilly, and I could feel that summer wasn't going to last forever. I shivered and put on a pair of heavy cotton socks. The dreary quiet of the morning matched my gloomy mood.

Instead of answering, Amy tiptoed into the living room with a finger over her mouth, hushing me. Through the door I could see Grandpa on the fold-out couch, still asleep, snoring gently. Amy crept past him with exaggerated caution, and I followed her into the kitchen.

Aunt Kate was leaning against the counter, holding a cup of tea in both hands, her hair braided into two long ropes like a little girl's.

"Morning, Alice," she said softly. "You slept late. I'm sorry Amy woke you up, but she really wanted to. I thought if I didn't let her, she'd cry and wake up Grandpa."

"That's okay," I whispered. "I'm not tired. I got plenty of sleep." Another lie. But who was counting? I hid a yawn and opened the refrigerator door, looking for breakfast. Amy banged through the kitchen door and ran out onto the porch, her pink sneakers pounding loudly on the floorboards.

"Shhh, Amy, Grandpa's sleeping," Aunt Kate hissed through the screen. She turned to me, frowning, and whispered, "Grandpa didn't get in till 3:00 A.M. He's too old for hours like this. He ought to stop delivering babies. I think I'd better take Amy out someplace for a while so that he can get some more sleep."

"I'll take her," I whispered back, closing the refrigerator again. "We'll go out in the woods. You can stay here, Aunt Kate. You can paint."

Aunt Kate fiddled with the end of a braid. "Well, I don't have to paint every day, you know. And I think I've been working you too hard, Alice. You have circles under your eyes, and you've been awfully quiet lately."

"I'm fine, Aunt Kate, really," I said. "Don't worry about me. You stay here."

Aunt Kate still looked worried. "I was going to pick some blueberries to take up to the neighbors' for dinner tonight. Why don't we all do that together?"

But I could hardly wait to escape to the hideout, where, maybe, I would be able to think. I grabbed a bagel out of the bread box and forced a cheerful smile for Aunt Kate. "No thanks! I'll take Amy out in the woods for a while, and you'll be able to pick berries in peace. See you later!" I said, and fled through the screen door before Aunt Kate could argue with me anymore.

It was a relief to get outside, where dark clouds hung overhead, and the air was soft and heavy with the feel of approaching rain. I let the fake smile fade from my face. "Come on, Amy, let's go to the hideout," I called.

"Okay!" Amy never needed urging to go there. She ran toward the beginning of the trail at the edge of the yard. I followed her, chewing on my bagel, thinking hard. There had to be some way I could stop this dinner at the Bird House from happening. But how?

Amy ran ahead of me up the path. She seemed to know the way to the hideout all by herself now. When she came to the fallen tree that marked the spot where the turn was to the shack, she left the path without glancing back at me and climbed nimbly onto the log.

"Wait for me, Amy," I called, and broke into a run. It was when I caught up with her that the idea came to me.

I grabbed her hand and stood still, balanced on top of the rotten log, staring blindly at a clump of ferns growing at the foot of a white birch tree. Maybe it would work. It might work, anyway. It couldn't hurt to try.

"Come on, Alice," Amy tugged impatiently at my hand. "Hurry up."

"Wait a minute, Amy," I said slowly. "Let's not go to the hideout after all. Let's go up to the Bird House."

I turned around and pulled her after me, over the log

and back the way we had come. "No!" wailed Amy. "I want to go to my bunny house! No, no, no!"

I tried to ignore her and just pull her down the path, but she set her little heels into the dirt and resisted with surprising strength. I tugged again, and Amy burst into tears. I stopped and picked her up.

"Come on, Amy, please don't cry," I begged. "I'll bring you back later, I promise. But there's something important I have to do. Let's go see the duckies, okay?"

"Duckies? Duckies . . ." Amy sniffled doubtfully. She didn't smile, but she stopped crying and let me carry her back through the woods, past the quiet cabin, and up the lane. It wasn't raining yet, but it was going to, any minute. The sky was dark, and the wind rustled through the trees and made the orange plastic butterfly on the porch at the Bird House rock as if it were trying to take off and fly away.

I thought we'd find Miss Abby in the yard, painting the house or gardening or fooling around with her lawn ornaments. But she wasn't there. Maybe she was in the backyard, I thought. She must be out here someplace. She was never indoors in the morning.

Amy wiggled down from my arms. "Hi, duckies," she yelled as if she were greeting old friends. She ran across the grass and sat down happily beside the row of marching yellow ducklings.

"Come inside with me, Amy," I called from the porch steps.

"No." Amy stuck out her lower lip. "I stay here. I see the ducks."

"Amy, it's going to rain any minute. And there's nobody here to watch you," I said impatiently.

But she just sat there, frowning, her lower lip trembling dangerously. She looked the way she had the day she'd thrown that tantrum. If I made her come in now, after I had already stopped her from going to the hideout, she'd have another one, I could tell, and Aunt Kate wasn't here to handle it for me. Where was Miss Abby, anyway? I had been counting on her to watch Amy, the way she had before, while I did what I had come to do. She must be in the house, I thought.

"I stay here," repeated Amy stubbornly.

"Oh, okay," I said. "I'll find Miss Abby and tell her you're out here. She'll be along in a minute, I bet. But *stay* there, okay?"

"Okay," said Amy, with her sweetest smile. I turned away from her to knock on the door.

Madame Merlina opened it almost right away.

"Hi, Madame Merlina," I said hurriedly, looking around for Miss Abby. She wasn't anywhere in sight.

"Why, hello, child." Madame Merlina looked surprised to see me, but not exactly glad. There was something troubled in her face, but I didn't wait to find out what it was.

"Madame Merlina, is Miss Abby around?" I asked quickly.

"No, she is not here," answered Madame Merlina, that strange look still on her face. "She has gone to Davenport's, to buy groceries for tonight's dinner. Why do you ask?"

"Oh, never mind." I sighed in frustration, glancing back outside. Miss Abby's car was gone from the driveway; I should have noticed that before. Amy was still sitting happily on the grass, patting a plastic duck and singing to herself. I would just have to do this fast, I thought. At least it wasn't raining yet.

Madame Merlina cleared her throat. "Alice, child, I am glad you have come. I hoped for an opportunity to speak with you."

But I cut her off. "We have to do the Ouija board, Madame Merlina. We have to do it right away." I stepped past her and hurried across the living room to the alcove. The Ouija board was in its usual place on the table, the unlit candle waiting beside it in its brass holder. I sat down in one of the carved chairs. But Madame Merlina just stood there in the middle of the living room, frowning worriedly at me.

"Perhaps we shouldn't," she said. "I—I do not know just what happened yesterday, Alice, but you seemed very distressed. Sometimes—sometimes spiritual things can be dangerous, you know. It is a serious matter, and—well, I wonder if we should wait a little before we attempt to communicate with the spirits again."

"Oh, no," I said, shocked. "Oh, Madame Merlina, we *have* to use the Ouija board. We have to contact Princess Owla, right now."

"We have to? What do you mean, child?"

"Well, I had—I had a message from Princess Owla, in the night," I invented recklessly. "She said she had to speak to us this morning on the Ouija board. She said it was very important."

"What kind of message?" Madame Merlina was still frowning.

"She just spoke to me. It was—it was in a dream. Oh, Madame Merlina, we just have to, that's all. Please!" I was in an agony of impatience.

Madame Merlina came reluctantly over and sat down across from me.

"Well, I suppose if we are careful," she said thoughtfully. "You seem to think this is very important. But Alice, if you start to feel—well, bothered, or disturbed, again, you must tell me, and we will stop right away."

"Of course, of course." I tapped my fingers anxiously on the planchette, and then jumped back up again and crossed to one of the living room windows to check on Amy. I had to push aside ivy tendrils to see outside, but there she was, sitting safely in the grass where I'd left her, rocking her bunny. I could just hear her small voice, singing off-key.

I sat back down, relieved. Madame Merlina seemed to move more slowly than she ever had before, deliberately striking a match, lighting the candle, settling herself in the chair, placing her fingers carefully on the planchette, closing her eyes and sitting motionless for what seemed like an eternity. I thought she would never ask that first question.

But at last she did. "Princess Owla," she said, in that strange, dreamy monotone she used only for the Ouija board. "Do you have some message for us?"

I pushed the planchette across the board so eagerly that Madame Merlina's fingers almost slipped off it. *"Yes."* I read the words out loud. *"I B-R-I-N-G A W-A-R-N-I-N-G."*

Madame Merlina opened her eyes and blinked at the board in surprise. "A warning? What sort of warning?"

"K-E-E-P S-I-L-E-N-C-E," I made the board spell. I read the words I was spelling out loud, speaking slowly,

trying to make my voice sound deep and commanding. *"T-E-L-L N-O-B-O-D-Y A-B-O-U-T M-E."*

"Tell nobody about you?" repeated Madame Merlina. "Princess Owla, I do not understand. Do you mean we should not reveal our contacts with you?"

"Y-E-S," I spelled. *"B-E S-I-L-E-N-T. S-A-Y N-O-T-H-I-N-G O-F O-U-R C-O-N-T-A-C-T T-O A-N-Y-B-O-D-Y."* I stopped talking and sat back, as out of breath as if I'd run a mile.

"Why—my goodness," said Madame Merlina slowly. "I never heard of such a request before. Princess Owla, what is the danger? Are you still there? Alice, what are you doing?"

I had lifted my fingers off the planchette. While I had been concentrating on the Princess Owla's warning, I had forgotten for a few minutes about Amy, all by herself out in the yard. I listened hard; I couldn't hear her singing anymore. How long had it been since I'd looked out that window and checked on her?

I got up and went back to the window, lifting a tendril of ivy out of the way. Outside, it was darker than it had been before, and the blades of the windmill spun in the wind. Amy was no longer sitting where I had left her, nor could I see her in the small slice of yard visible through the ivy leaves.

"Oh, no," I whispered, and ran across the room to the door, my spine suddenly as cold as if someone had dropped an ice cube down my shirt.

"Alice, come back," called Madame Merlina behind me, sounding more confused than angry. "We have not finished. Where are you going?"

But I was already at the door, pulling it open, knowing

with cold, awful certainty what I would see. "Amy," I said in a small voice. "Where's Amy?"

But nobody answered. The rising wind rattled the plastic butterfly, thump, thump, thump, against the porch, and the pinwheel wings of the wooden ducks spun with a thin clattering sound. The flamingo and the plastic ducklings and the glaring owl stood motionless among the flowers. Nothing living moved in the yard. There was no sign of Amy at all.

16

"Amy!" I yelled. But the wind blew my voice away.

I didn't wait to explain anything to Madame Merlina. I leaped across the porch, down the steps, and through the yard, yelling Amy's name, running as fast as I could go back toward the cabin.

She must have gone back there, I told myself. She wouldn't have gone into the woods, the endless woods, that crowded close to the road, branches lashing in the rising wind. I ran breathlessly around the curve in the road just before the cabin, hoping to see her ahead of me, trotting down the lane in her little pink sneakers.

But Amy wasn't there. The porch was empty, the yard was still. The glider swing swayed a little in the wind, and Amy's sand toys lay scattered under the beech tree where she'd left them the day before. As I ran toward the cabin, Aunt Kate emerged through the pine trees from the blueberry patch, carrying Grandpa's canvas hat upside down in front of her.

"Hi, Alice," she called to me. "I got plenty of berries, and just in time—it's going to pour any minute!"

Then, as I got close enough for her to see my expression, she stopped short.

"Alice, where's Amy?" Watching me, she let the hat tip a little, and some berries spilled over the brim.

"I don't know—" I panted. "I—I was hoping she was here—isn't she here?"

Aunt Kate stood perfectly still for a moment, staring at me. Then she dropped the hat, berries bouncing everywhere, and ran across the yard to the cabin. She leaped up the porch steps and disappeared inside, the screen door slamming behind her with a hollow bang.

"Dad?" I heard her call. "Is Amy with you?"

A moment later she burst back out onto the porch with Grandpa behind her, shaving cream on his chin and a towel in his hand. From where I stood at the foot of the porch steps, I could see the freckles on Aunt Kate's cheekbones standing out as clearly as if she'd been sprinkled with cinnamon.

"She isn't inside," Aunt Kate said. "My God, Alice, where is she?"

I opened my mouth, but I couldn't say anything. My voice seemed to have dried up in my throat. Grandpa stepped past Aunt Kate, wiping the shaving cream off his jaw with the towel.

"Alice," he said. "Was Amy with you?"

I nodded dumbly.

He came down the steps and put a gentle hand on my shoulder. "Where were you, honey? Where did you see her last?"

"Up at the Bird House," I croaked. "She was in the yard—I only went inside for a few minutes. When I came out, she was gone."

"How long has she been gone?"

"I—I don't know," I stammered. "I'm not really sure how long I was in there."

Grandpa's hand tightened on my shoulder until it began to hurt. "Alice," he said, and his voice was so gentle that it was terrible. "Did you look for her at the pond?"

But my voice was gone again. Slowly, I shook my head, staring up at Grandpa. He let go of my shoulder and turned away from me, his shoulders sagging so that he looked, suddenly, very old.

"Katie, I'll get right up to the pond. But first maybe we'd better call the sheriff," he said. "If she's in the woods, we'll need some help looking for her."

I didn't wait for Aunt Kate to say anything. I turned away from their two white faces and started to run back up the lane the way I had come. The pond! Why hadn't I checked there first? It was so close to the Bird House. She could easily have wandered over there while I was wasting time running back to the cabin.

I closed my mind on what could have happened to Amy if she had gone to the pond and just ran, back up the lane, past the Bird House, where Miss Abby was getting out of her car and Madame Merlina was a vague dark shape on the porch. I ran past them without a word, into the field and across the growing hay to where the pond lay by the willow tree.

"Amy!" I jumped up onto the dreaming rock, shading my eyes with my hand so that I could see better, probing the bank and the waving clumps of reeds for a glimpse of her dark curls. "Amy, are you here? Amy! Amy!"

But nobody answered except a blackbird hovering over my head, scolding frantically because I was too close to its nest. The pond was as quiet and lovely as ever, the water dark with reflected storm clouds, its silent surface rippling in the wind. She could be down under there and nobody would know, I thought, and then drove the idea out of my mind. She wasn't in the pond, she couldn't be. Pushing down panic that rose inside me like sobs, I turned my back on the silent water and ran across the hay field to the Bird House.

Miss Abby was on the porch with a grocery bag in her arms when I pounded up the steps. Madame Merlina had disappeared. "Merlina says Amy's lost," she greeted me. "How long has she been gone?"

"Not long," I panted, although it seemed to me already that Amy had been lost for hours. "Ten minutes, maybe fifteen."

"Well, then, she can't have come to much harm," said Miss Abby briskly. She sounded so efficient and comforting that all of a sudden she reminded me overwhelmingly of my mother.

"Oh, Miss Abby, it's all my fault," I wailed.

But she didn't try to comfort me. "That doesn't matter now," she told me firmly, handing the grocery bag to me. "What's important is to find her. Now, Alice, listen. I'll go right down to your family's house and see how I can help. Just take this sack inside and tell my sister to wait here in case Amy comes back. Then you'd better go home, too, quick as you can."

"Okay," I said reluctantly. I wanted to go with her; I wanted to search for Amy, everywhere, all at once, without wasting another minute. But I stood there helplessly, watching Miss Abby as she hurried down the steps, climbed into her car, started it up, and backed out of the yard without another glance at me.

Without knocking, I ran into the Bird House, blinking in the green dimness. There in the alcove was Madame Merlina, sitting at the table with the candle burning, just as if it were an ordinary day and she was ready for another session with the princess Owla.

Suddenly all my fear changed into fury. "What are you doing? Aren't you going to help look for Amy?" I burst out at her.

She stared at me, her pale eyes wide and defenseless. When she spoke, her voice was shaking. "I am trying to help, child. I have looked in the shed, and I started down toward the pond, but I cannot see very well, as you know. And then it came to me that I was wasting time, and I realized what we must do. Come sit down, Alice. We must ask the Ouija board where Amy is."

"No, no," I cried. "There's no time for that. We have to go look for her!"

"But we must," said Madame Merlina. "You are a medium, my child. You have the ability. It would be a waste of time not to use it. And we may have no time to lose."

I opened my mouth to explain that I was not a medium and never had been, that I was a liar and the Ouija board was nonsense and nothing but searching would find Amy. But then I saw the quaver in Madame Merlina's old hands as she placed the planchette on the board, and the way her beaked nose seemed to stand out more sharply from her face than it normally did. She looked, all at once, very old and very frightened. Could she actually be worried about Amy? I hadn't thought she cared about anyone but her stupid old spirits.

I swallowed hard, stifled my rising panic, set down the

bag of groceries, and placed my fingers on the planchette opposite hers. It will only take a minute, I told myself. And maybe it will make Madame Merlina feel better.

"Oh, spirits, where is the child?" asked Madame Merlina. It didn't occur to me to push the planchette. I wasn't even paying attention. I was staring over her shoulder, seeing, instead of the dim alcove, the rippling surface of the pond, so quiet, so scary. I yearned with every bit of myself to see, instead, Amy's small face, alive and dirty and not drowned in pond water or lost in the endless woods. Where could she have gone?

"Spirits!" repeated Madame Merlina loudly. "Where is the child?"

I stared down at the planchette, motionless on the polished board. Maybe, if I concentrated hard enough, the Ouija board would really work. Something had moved it that first time, after all, and even Grandpa had said that maybe there really were spirits. Maybe it was worth trying. I closed my eyes and concentrated as hard as I could on Amy, picturing her small face with its impish grin and that wild, dark wreath of curly hair, trying to push my thoughts down through my fingertips. Where is she? I asked silently. Help us find her. Please.

But the planchette didn't move. Madame Merlina spoke again.

"Spirits, where is Amy? Where is the child?"

The candle flame flickered. I could hear the blackbirds calling outside by the pond. Nothing happened.

Then, for just a moment, the planchette seemed to quiver. I caught my breath, and Madame Merlina glanced up at me, her eyes bright with hope. But the quivering stopped, and the planchette stood still again. Maybe it was the trembling of Madame Merlina's fingers that had made it shake.

We stared at the motionless planchette for another moment, and then Madame Merlina looked at me. Her face was creased with worry.

"I do not understand," she said. "Why are the spirits silent? Why doesn't it move?"

Something seemed to lurch inside me. All at once I pulled my fingers off the planchette.

"Madame Merlina, it isn't going to move," I said. "Not unless I push it."

She blinked at me. "What do you mean?"

"I mean, there aren't any spirits, or at least, not here." I was reckless with guilt and worry. "I'm not a medium. I've been pushing this thing all this time, making up all those stories about Atlantis. The Ouija board can't help us find Amy."

"You made it all up?"

"I made it up, Madame Merlina. I lied to you." My heart was thumping so hard I thought it would break right out through my T-shirt. "I got started, and then I didn't know how to stop. I—I didn't really mean to."

Madame Merlina wasn't looking at me anymore. She was staring down at the Ouija board as if it had bitten her. "None of that was real?" Her thin old voice was soft and wondering. "Not Atlantis, or the dancer, or any of it?"

I swallowed hard and made myself answer her. "None of it. I made it all up."

"Even the log castle? The secret place?" She was looking

at me again, and her faded old eyes seemed to be begging me for something. "That was my favorite part."

"Well," I said, "I didn't completely make that part up. It isn't in Atlantis, but it is real. It's here, near the cabin, in the woods—"

I stopped in the middle of a breath. A picture of Amy was forming in my mind, as vivid as the wrinkled face of Madame Merlina in front of me. She was standing on the hollow log, tugging against my hand holding hers, and she was hollering. "No, no, no!" she yelled in my vision. "Alice, I want to go to my bunny house!"

I jumped up so fast that the Ouija board clattered onto the floor. "I have to go," I stammered breathlessly. "I think I know where Amy is. I have to go right now!"

I dashed out the front door. Madame Merlina followed me, calling, "Wait! I want to help you look for the child! Have you called the sheriff?"

"Grandpa did!" I yelled, and I bolted away from her across the yard.

As I ran down the lane I could hear Aunt Kate and Grandpa calling Amy's name from down by the pond, their voices thin and lost-sounding. The faraway howl of a siren rose from the valley. I kept going, running past the cabin to the Indian trail. Branches lashed at my face and I tripped over rocks, but I didn't slow down.

I pounded breathlessly along the path, watching for the rotten log. It didn't take long to get there; it wouldn't be too far for Amy to go, I thought, even all by herself. I veered off the trail and jumped over the log. Here was the faint path zigzagging through the birch trees. The hideout was just ahead, masked by the clump of trees.

"Amy? Amy!" I dashed through the trees. There was the dark shape of the hideout, shadowy in the dim light under the trees. It looked different, somehow, but I ran right up to it before I saw the reason.

It had collapsed. What had been a rickety structure standing higher than my head was now just a jumbled heap of logs and drying-up pine branches. And protruding between two of them, near the bottom, were the dirty pink plush ears of Amy's bunny.

17

All I remember of the next few minutes are flashes: pine needles scattering as I tossed the roof branches aside, rough bark scratching my hands as I tugged at the logs, the crack of a pole rolling off the pile into my shin, and the sound of my own ragged voice yelling, "Amy! Amy!" And the worst sound of all: utter silence from under the pile of logs. No little girl's voice, no sobs, no sounds of life.

The poles weren't heavy, but they were tangled together like giant pick-up sticks. It seemed to take a year to disentangle each one and drag it away from the pile. But at last I lifted away a peeling birch log, thicker than the others, and exposed a dark space inside the pile. It was hollow, and, at my first terrified glimpse within, empty. "Amy!" I yelled again, and something in the darkness moved. There, glimmering up at me through the dimness like a pale rock under pond water, was a small face.

It almost didn't seem to be Amy. She was crouching in a corner that, by some miracle, had not collapsed along with the rest. Her eyes were blank and shocked, showing, at first, no sign that she knew me. I had time to notice that blood was spattered across her forehead and cheek. Then her face suddenly crumpled and she was unmistakably Amy, wailing, "Get my bunny out! My bunny is stuck! Alice, get my bunny out!"

I started to reach for her to pull her out through the

opening I had created. But as my hands found her shoulders, I froze. The voice of some first-aid teacher in Girl Scouts seemed to speak in my ear: Never move a person after an accident. You might make an injury worse.

Amy was howling now, stretching her small hands up through the hole. I stared down at her, paralyzed with doubt. If her back was hurt, or she had a broken bone, I might make it worse if I lifted her out. But I couldn't leave her there alone in that black hole in the logs while I went for help.

As I stood there worrying, Amy decided the question for me. She struggled to her feet, trying to grab me through the hole, and her shoulder banged against the logs. A couple of poles tumbled off the top, and the remaining heap surrounding Amy shifted ominously.

I stopped debating, got a grip under her arms, and pulled her out, dirty, draped with cobwebs, wonderfully alive and wiggly in my arms. She smelled of baby shampoo and blood.

She touched my cheek and said, in her ordinary voice, "Hello, Alice. I was stuck!" Then her face crumpled again. She twisted away from me, back toward the pile of logs, and yelled, "I want my bunny!"

"Okay, honey, hang on, I'll get it for you." I hoped that I could. Holding Amy on my hip, I tugged at the bunny ears where they stuck out from the logs, but they didn't budge. I leaned over the pile, stuck my arm back into the hole, fished around until I felt the furry body inside, and yanked. The bunny pulled free and I grabbed it away as the rest of the pile of logs collapsed, tumbling onto the ground. Poles bumped against my ankles and rolled among the trees as I scrambled away, handing the damp, dirty bunny to Amy.

"Poor bunny, was you stuck?" Her clear voice sounded completely normal as she tucked the bunny up against her cheek and popped her thumb into her mouth. I looked her over feverishly as I lugged her through the woods. The blood on her face came from a cut on top of her head. Her hair was matted and sticky, hiding the cut so that I couldn't see how big it was, but it didn't seem to be bleeding anymore. She was moving her arms and legs as if they were all right. Except for some scratches here and there, I couldn't see anything else wrong with her.

As I stepped over the rotten log, rain began to patter through the leaves and then fell hard, tracing cool ribbons through the dust and sweat on my face. I tried to keep Amy's head dry with my hand. The wild pounding of my heart was beginning to ease, but my legs were shaky, and my ankles ached where the logs had banged into them. Amy's weight made me awkward, and I slipped and stumbled as the dirt path turned slick in the rain.

Thunder rumbled overhead as we got to the edge of the woods. In the yard stood a police car, dome light blinking. Huddled close together beside it, ignoring the downpour, were the Bird sisters, two police officers, and Grandpa, with Aunt Kate leaning against him as if she had no strength left of her own. At first none of them noticed Amy and me.

But Amy saw them. She came suddenly to life in my arms, wriggling like a just-hooked fish. I set her down just as Aunt Kate looked up and saw us.

"Mommy!" yelled Amy, pelting toward her. "My bunny was stuck!"

Aunt Kate took a couple of steps, dropped to her knees and reached out, and Amy ran into her arms.

They stayed like that for a moment, so closely entangled that they were more like one person than two. Grandpa stood behind them, looking over their heads at me. Even through his glasses and the rain, his eyes shone like a beacon.

Then Miss Abby was hugging me, her big, soft arms closing out the wild and rainy world. She smelled powdery and warm, like my mother. Over her shoulder, I caught a quick glimpse of Madame Merlina, her white hair flattened down around her head by the rain, watching me with no expression at all on her face. But then Miss Abby tightened her arms around me, and in her embrace I couldn't see anyone anymore.

In the middle of that night, I came suddenly awake. My room was dark, and my covers were in a tangled knot at the foot of my bed. I could hear Grandpa moving quietly around the living room. He'd said, the evening before, that he'd check on Amy a few times during the night. He had talked with another doctor on the phone, and they had decided that she didn't have to have X rays. The cut on her head didn't need stitches, and the bump was small. But still, Grandpa had said, the only way to be absolutely sure she didn't have a dangerous head injury would be to wake her up every few hours during the night.

I listened to the floorboards creak as Grandpa moved into Amy's room. I could hear Grandpa's and Aunt Kate's low voices, murmuring on the other side of the wall, but I didn't hear Amy.

It's all my fault, I thought. I turned wretchedly onto my

back and stared up into the darkness. It seemed to be full of pictures: Grandpa's gray face as he'd gripped my shoulder; the Ouija board, motionless as I silently begged it to tell me where Amy was; Amy's bunny, caught in the tumbled logs; Madame Merlina's face, thin and defenseless in the rain.

I pulled my pillow out from under my head and covered my face with it, trying to block out the awful pictures. Then I pulled it off again so that I could listen for Amy's voice through the wall, but I couldn't hear anything.

She'll be fine, I told myself. Grandpa had almost promised she would be, the night before. It was just a little cut, he had said. There was hardly even a lump on her head. But he had wanted to keep her quiet, so we hadn't gone to the Bird House for dinner after all. Miss Abby had said we could do it another time, when we'd all calmed down a little.

Well, that was what I wanted, I thought bitterly. I had wanted to stop the party, and I had certainly succeeded. But I hadn't meant for it to happen like this.

Grandpa's voice rumbled through the wall. Still no sound from Amy. It's all my fault, I thought again. Nobody had said so last night. Neither Grandpa nor Aunt Kate had scolded me for losing Amy, or punished me, or said very much about it at all, though Aunt Kate had thanked me for finding her. They'd concentrated on taking care of Amy, and they had left me pretty much alone.

I wished they had punished me. I'd outgrown spankings long ago—my parents never really believed in spanking, anyway. But I wanted something—a scolding, or a grounding, or some kind of punishment—to help me get rid of the awful weight of guilt inside.

Of course, nobody knew just how badly I needed punishing. I hadn't told Grandpa and Aunt Kate the whole story of how I'd lost Amy. All they knew was that I'd gone into the Bird House for a while without her. They didn't know why. They knew about the hideout, now, of course. But they didn't know about the Ouija board, or Atlantis, or Princess Owla. They didn't know about me.

All of a sudden I couldn't lie there in the dark anymore. I jumped out of bed and stumbled across my room, groping in the darkness for the doorknob.

As I came, blinking, into the lit-up living room, Grandpa stepped through Aunt Kate's door, yawning. He was still fully dressed.

"Grandpa, is Amy okay?" I asked.

"She's fine, sweetheart," he said. His face looked different at night, crumpled and tired. Older. I had never thought about how old Grandpa was before. Now, looking at him, I couldn't help seeing it. "You should be asleep, Alice Anne," he said. "It's after midnight."

"I can't sleep," I said. Through the half-open door behind Grandpa, I could see Aunt Kate in the rocking chair beside Amy's crib, a bar of light from the living room falling across her face. Grandpa turned back to her.

"You don't have to stay up with her, Katie. Go to bed," he said softly.

"Thanks, Dad." Aunt Kate's voice from the darkness was even softer than Grandpa's. "I'll just sit with her a little longer."

Grandpa patted her shoulder. Then he came over to where I stood beside the fireplace. A few coals still glowed on the hearth from the fire he'd built earlier. He didn't say anything, and the quiet stretched out between us.

Finally, I spoke into the silence. "Grandpa, would you take a walk with me?"

"Aren't you tired, Alice Anne?"

"Not very," I said. It wasn't exactly true that I wasn't tired. I seemed to ache everywhere, bones and muscles and bruised ankles. But something inside of me seemed to be humming, a high, anxious kind of whine, like a plane getting ready to take off or a bomb waiting to explode. I didn't want to go back into my dark room alone.

"Well, I can't sleep, either," admitted Grandpa. "Moon's out, too. Come on, then, let's go up to the pond."

I pulled a jacket on over my nightgown and slipped my bare feet into my sneakers. As we stepped out of the cabin, the wind grabbed at us as if to pull us with it into the sky. The rain had stopped, and the storm was blowing away. A round silver moon rode high behind tatters of cloud. Trees bent and rustled, and the wind tugged at my hair and moaned, sounding as desolate as I felt.

I held Grandpa's hand as if it were a lifeline as we pushed our way silently against the wind, up the lane and past the Bird House, where a solitary second-floor light burned through the darkness, and across the hay field to the blackbird pond.

We walked along the bank to the willow tree and sat down together on the dreaming rock. The pond water slapped restlessly against the banks. The moon's reflection was broken up by the little waves, scattered across the surface like pieces of shattered glass.

Suddenly, from the branches of the willow, just above our heads, a wild shriek rose above the wind. I grabbed Grandpa. It was a crazy, high, warbling screech, like a ghost or a wild man, the worst noise I'd ever heard. I shrieked, too, and burst into tears. But Grandpa was laughing and pointing at a soft shape flapping silently away from the tree.

"It's a screech owl, that's all," he said, putting an arm around my shoulders. "Just a screech owl yelling at us. Sounds awful, but won't kill us. It's okay, Alice. Calm down, honey."

But I couldn't calm down. The shock of that screech had seemed to break something inside me. I hadn't let myself cry since I'd found Amy, and now that I had started, I couldn't stop. I buried my face in Grandpa's shirt and howled.

He just patted my back and waited. After a while the first wild storm of crying subsided a little and I started to snuffle and gasp. Grandpa pulled a handkerchief out of the pocket of his corduroy jacket and handed it to me.

"Glad the waterworks are slowing down a little. Wouldn't want you to flood the pond," he said, and I managed a soggy smile. He didn't smile back. He was gazing down at me, and the moonlight shone on his glasses so that I couldn't quite see his eyes. "Want to tell me what's on your mind?" he said.

I didn't want to, not at all. But I knew that he knew it wasn't just the owl that had made me cry, and something in the watchful stillness of his face in the moonlight told me that he knew it wasn't just what had happened to Amy, either. I held his hand and took a deep breath, still shuddery with crying.

"I told a lie, Grandpa," I said, and watched his face anxiously. It didn't change. "A big lie, a bunch of lies. I've been telling a lot of lies, all summer long."

And after that, the whole story tumbled out, while

162

Grandpa sat still and listened. I told him how it had started, the day that Amy found her way into the Bird House, and Madame Merlina had seemed so grouchy and strange that I didn't feel bad about fooling her. And I told him how once I did start feeling bad, I didn't know how to stop the lie I'd started, and I just had to keep on lying and lying and feeling worse and worse. I told him about the lies I'd told Aunt Kate, too, about drawing and about losing Amy the first time. And then I told him how it had happened that Amy had disappeared, and I thought I would start crying again. But I didn't. Somehow while I talked, all the sobs had gone from inside me, replaced by a tired, aching kind of peace.

I couldn't read Grandpa's face in the moonlight. I couldn't tell if he was angry. But his hand was warm on mine, and somehow it didn't matter. I had told him the truth, and something inside me that had been hurting all summer seemed to have stopped. I sat beside Grandpa in the moonlight and waited.

After a while his arm came around my shoulder. It felt good, and I cuddled into it.

"Guess you've got some apologizing to do," he said quietly.

"Apologizing?" I stammered. "To who?"

"To whom," said Grandpa. "You sound just like that owl. Didn't you plan on apologizing?"

"Well, yes," I said. "To you. And Aunt Kate, of course. I'll do that tomorrow, Grandpa, I promise."

"Is that all?" Grandpa's voice was gentle.

"Yes," I said, but I was afraid I knew what he was thinking.

"Are you sure?"

"Yes!" I muttered stubbornly.

Grandpa said nothing. His glasses glinted in the moonlight.

I pulled away from his warm arm. "You want me to apologize to Madame Merlina, don't you," I said.

Grandpa still said nothing.

"Oh, Grandpa, no!" I cried. "I can't go see Madame Merlina. I just can't. It's too embarrassing. I mean, I am sorry, I really am, but I don't want to go near her, ever again. I know you're mad at me, Grandpa, and I deserve it, but couldn't you just—just punish me or something?"

Grandpa sighed. "Mad isn't really the word for how I feel, Alice. Disappointed, yes, but not mad. And as far as punishment goes, it sounds to me as if you're doing a pretty good job of punishing yourself. That's not the problem. Miss Bird's a very lonely woman, honey. You have her feelings to think of."

I didn't answer right away. Over Grandpa's shoulder, across the hay field, I could see that single light burning in the Bird House. I was suddenly sure the light was Madame Merlina's.

"Couldn't I just write her a note?" I asked finally.

But Grandpa patted my shoulder. "Think you've got to do it face to face, sweetheart. She might have things she'd like to say to you, too, you know."

I stiffened my back and gulped. "Okay, okay," I said. "I'll go up there tomorrow morning."

"That's my girl." The warmth was back in Grandpa's voice. "Any more secrets you've been keeping from me?"

I thought of the sketchbook full of my drawings hidden under the mattress back at the cabin. "Well, yes," I said.

"There is one more. I've been learning to draw, Grandpa. At the hideout. I've been drawing a lot, all summer."

Grandpa's laugh rumbled softly beside me. "That doesn't sound too terrible."

"I guess not. But I didn't want to tell anybody." I struggled to explain why I'd wanted my drawings to be secret, but all of a sudden I felt so sleepy I couldn't think straight. "I did a picture of Amy. I think you'd like it—" I interrupted myself with a huge yawn.

Grandpa patted my shoulder again. "I want to see those pictures. Tomorrow morning, okay? Now, Alice Anne, we have more talking to do, you and me, about this lying and what that's all about. But it's late, and I'm tired, and you're about to fall over asleep into the pond. Let's head on back and check Amy one more time before bed."

Grandpa kept his arm around me all the way back to the cabin. I wanted to tell him how much I loved him, but from the way he looked at me as we stepped into the pool of light outside the cabin door, I could tell he already knew.

18

The next day the world was washed clean by the storm, damp and glittering in the new sunlight. I stood on the porch of the Bird House with a basket of blueberry muffins Grandpa had helped me make, trying to get up my courage to knock on the door. It was one thing to know that the only way I could make up for what I'd done was to go and tell Madame Merlina how sorry I was. But it was another thing to do it. My hand kept hiding in the pocket of my shorts, and I stood there shifting from foot to foot.

I don't know when I would have found the courage to knock. But unexpectedly, the door opened, and standing there was Miss Abby.

"Why, Alice, you're quiet as a mouse—I didn't hear you come onto the porch!" Her smile was as friendly as ever, and she talked so fast that I didn't have a chance to say anything. "You look tired, dear, but that isn't surprising. Oh, I'm glad you came up. Even after your grandfather called us last night to say Amy was all right, I don't think either of us slept much. How is she this morning?"

"She's fine, Miss Abby. She's great, in fact, running around and singing just like always," I said. "Um, is Madame Merlina—"

But Miss Abby kept on talking. "Thanks goodness that child's all right," she said. "What a scare that was. I smell

166

muffins—are those for us? Thank you! I was just going out to weed my flowers. Want to come?"

"Um, I came to talk to Madame Merlina, really," I said, fumbling with my basket. "I mean, it's not that I don't want to see you, but I have to talk to her—I have to, um, tell her something, um, I guess I should say, apologize to her for something." I stopped and twisted miserably at a button on my shirt. "The truth is, I told her a lie."

Miss Abby didn't look surprised. She came out the door, closed it behind her, and more or less shooed me ahead of her down the porch steps. "Come along, Alice. It'll keep a few minutes," she said.

I trotted along beside her as we crossed the yard to the petunia bed where the plastic owl stood guard. She walked surprisingly fast for a lady as heavy as she was.

Miss Abby squatted down by the petunias and tweaked out an invading dandelion. Without looking at me, she said, "You might not have as much to apologize for as you think, you know. Myrlene has always loved pretending."

I opened my mouth to argue with her and then stopped. "Did you say 'Myrlene'?"

"Myrlene," repeated Miss Abby firmly. "Yes, I did."

"But, why?" I asked. "That's not her name."

"Oh, yes, it is." The voice came from behind me, deep and unexpected. I dropped my basket of muffins in surprise as I turned. Madame Merlina was on the porch, a shadow against the yellow clapboards. "Madame Merlina!" I exclaimed. "Um, I didn't know you were here—I wanted to talk to you—" I was babbling, but she cut me off.

"My real name is Myrlene," she said. "I know you are here to see me, child. Not because the spirits told me; I heard you say so, through the window. I have things to say to you, too."

Miss Abby stood up and gave me a quick, reassuring smile. She picked up the basket of muffins and went up the steps onto the porch. As she passed Madame Merlina, she reached out and touched her shoulder lightly, and then she disappeared into the house.

Madame Merlina picked her way carefully down the steps and sat down on the bottom one. I noticed for the first time that she was carrying the Ouija board. She put it down beside her and beckoned to me.

Myrlene. I tried the taste of it silently on my tongue as I crossed the yard and sat down beside her. I wouldn't like to have that name myself, I thought. I didn't blame Madame Merlina—Myrlene—whatever her name was—for wanting to change it.

"I changed my name when I was a girl," she said suddenly, as if she knew what I was thinking. "Not much older than you. I hated *Myrlene*—I guess you can imagine why." Her face broke unexpectedly into a smile, a rather creaky one, as though it hadn't been used much. "Then I read in the name section of our dictionary that Merlina means 'black bird of night,' and I thought that sounded wonderful. So I decided to change my name."

I didn't say anything. Madame Merlina was gazing at some zinnias blooming beside the steps, as if she were looking through them to see something I couldn't. She didn't seem to be finished. After a minute, she started to talk again.

"Or at least I tried to change it. But Pa would not allow it—he forbade me to use any name but the one he gave me. He was an old-fashioned man, and very stern. He never did stand for any of my foolishness, as he used to call it. Well, I changed my name anyway. I made Abby call me Merlina when we were alone, but she couldn't, of course, when Pa was around." She laughed a little, softly. I don't think I had ever heard her laugh before. Her laugh was pretty. "I tried to get Abby to change her name, too. I was sure we could come up with something more spiritual. But she wouldn't. She said she liked the name she had."

She picked a zinnia and turned it over in her fingers, staring at it. "Oh, I had dreams for myself in those days. I was going to do such wonderful things, and Myrlene just wasn't the name to do them with. I swore that when I didn't live with Pa and Ma anymore, I'd never be Myrlene again."

"What—what wonderful things did you want to do?"

She laughed again, but this time her laugh sounded a little bitter. "It doesn't matter," she said. "I never did any of them. I had thought of becoming a dancer, but Pa would not allow me to take lessons, and after a while, I just stopped arguing with him. Well, we grew up, and Abby got a job and moved out to her own apartment, but somehow the right job for me never came along. None of the ones I could have had seemed as wonderful as my dreams. And then Ma died, and Pa got sick, and I had to take care of him. So that is what I did—for years and years. I lived right here. By the time Pa died—I don't know. I was growing old, I suppose. I didn't seem to have the spirit anymore to do those wonderful things. I couldn't even remember what they were. I moved in with Abby in Binghamton, and I began working for an insurance company. I did not enjoy the work, and then I began to have trouble with my eyes, and—well, I was not very happy. After a time, I became interested in spiritualism. It seemed to make things—well, less disappointing, I suppose."

She was silent for so long then that I got restless. I didn't want to interrupt. But I had come to apologize, and something odd was happening. Madame Merlina almost seemed to be apologizing to me.

"Madame Merlina—" I began hesitantly.

"Haven't you been listening, child?" she demanded, with a trace of her old bossiness. "That is not my name."

I cleared my throat nervously. "All right, Ma—I mean, Myr—anyway, I came to apologize. I lied to you, and I know—I know I hurt you. I'm very sorry."

"Oh, Alice." Unexpectedly, her dry old hand settled over mine, lightly, like a dead leaf landing. "There's more than one kind of lying. You were telling tall tales—dreaming out loud. The truth is, I suppose I never really believed you."

I was speechless for a minute. Then I croaked, "You didn't? But why didn't you say something?"

She patted my hand. "I liked it," she said. "I liked listening to you. That dream world of yours was wonderful. It reminded me—well, of myself, I suppose. Of the things I used to dream about. I didn't want you to stop. I suppose I was lying to myself—I pretended, even to myself, that I didn't know you were pushing that planchette."

"You were pretending, too?" I felt stung. Now I was the one who had been lied to.

"I am afraid I was, at least in part," she said soberly. "We will both have to stop that kind of pretending, I think. But we can keep dreaming, you know, young Alice. It's a terrible thing to stop dreaming. You have reminded me how to dream, and I am very glad of that."

Her bony hand tightened gently over mine. Then she smiled at me. Her smile looked a little less creaky already; maybe she was getting used to smiling. Or maybe I was just getting used to seeing it. She held the scarlet zinnia she'd been fiddling with up before her eyes and squinted at it.

"I have been wondering about gardening," she said, as if it were connected to the things she had been saying. "I have never tried to grow anything. It seemed such a mundane thing to do. Not spiritual enough, I suppose." To my utter astonishment, she winked at me.

"But I believe I may have been wrong." She handed the zinnia to me. "Vegetables would be good, I think. Yes, I believe I will plant a vegetable garden. Peas, maybe, and tomatoes, and squash. I can't see the dratted flowers very well, and Abby's the flower expert, anyway. But I can get my hands around vegetables. I can feel them, and I can smell them, and I can cook them. I am an excellent cook, though I do not believe I have ever told you so before."

"I like to cook, too," I heard myself say, to my own surprise. "I make very good blueberry pie."

"Well, perhaps someday you will agree to share your recipe with me." Madame Merlina gave me a hesitant, sideways look. "If you would like to, that is."

"Well, okay. I mean, yes, of course, I'd like that very much," I stammered, still a little confused.

Madame Merlina picked up the Ouija board and put it in my lap. "Here, child," she said. "I want you to have this."

"Oh, no!" I protested, pushing it back toward her. "I don't want to use that thing anymore."

"You do not have to use it," she said. "Throw it into the pond, if you want to. But I do not want it anymore, and it seems to me you should have it."

"Well, okay, I guess," I said reluctantly. "Thanks, Madame Merlina."

"I have already told you. That is not my name!" She rapped it out, in her old imperious voice.

"Well, it is to me," I said. "I can't help it, I can't start calling you Myrlene. Do you mind if I just go on calling you Madame Merlina?"

"Why, no." Her fierce old face softened again into that unexpectedly gentle smile. "I suppose I do not mind. As long as you will keep coming to see me, when you are here in the summer."

"Of course I will," I said. "Are—are you sure you want me to, though? I mean, after all this." I gestured at the Ouija board, lying half on her lap, half on mine.

"Do not be ridiculous, child." She scowled at me, her eyebrows bristling as ferociously as ever. "I would not say it if I did not mean it."

I found myself grinning at her. The Ouija board in its polished oak box lay between us, balanced on our knees, like a bridge connecting us to each other. Even though she was still frowning at me, even though she was so much older than I was, I suddenly saw that Madame Merlina was my friend. She had seen so much that was bad about me, but she must have seen something else, something good. Whatever she had seen, I could see that she liked me, and I realized with a rush of surprise that I liked her, too. We sat there, the Ouija board linking us, and even though we didn't speak, each of us knew what the other was thinking, as clearly as if we could read each other's minds.

Later that day Grandpa, Aunt Kate, Amy, and I went out together for a walk so that I could apologize to Aunt Kate. Telling her the truth about everything that had happened was hard, but Grandpa walked along beside me, saying nothing, helping just by being there. Aunt Kate listened quietly, her face serious, while I told her about the first time I'd lost Amy and explained exactly how I had lost her again the second time. But when I swallowed hard and told her about the art contest, she startled me by laughing out loud.

"Alice, you goose," she said. "Why did you ever think you needed to fib about being able to draw?"

"I don't know," I stammered. "I was afraid you'd think I was boring. I wanted you to admire me, I guess."

"Oh, Alice," she said. "I do, believe me. I admire you because you're wonderful with Amy. And because you're funny, and your imagination is a delight. And because you remind me of your mother when she was your age, and that's a constant joy. But Alice, you're special because of who you *are*, not because of what you can do. Who cares if you can draw?"

"Seems to me that you might be able to draw pretty well, someday," Grandpa put in. He had Amy up on his shoulders, where she was tugging eagerly at a few strands of his thin gray hair. "Those pictures you showed us today were pretty good, I thought."

"Oh, Grandpa, you're just biased," I said, but I could feel the color rising in my cheeks.

"Well, why not, Alice?" said Aunt Kate. "It'll take work, and faith in yourself, but I think you could be quite good if you choose to be."

I was silenced by that. We walked quietly along together till we came to the pond, where swallows skimmed so close to the water that ripples raced away from their wingtips across the silvery surface. I took a deep breath, happy to be back at the pond again. I hadn't realized just how much I'd missed it. I didn't have the hideout anymore, now that it had collapsed, but maybe I didn't need it. The blackbird pond had always been my special place. Now it could be again, because I didn't have to hide anymore.

I watched the quiet water reflect the sky and thought about throwing the Ouija board into the pond as Madame Merlina had suggested. I could picture how it would sail out over the surface, that narrow dark box reflected in the water below it, and hit in the middle, disappearing with a splash, leaving nothing behind it but widening circles.

But maybe I wouldn't. Maybe I'd keep it, for remembering. I still wondered about that first time, when the planchette had moved and neither Madame Merlina nor I had pushed it. I still didn't know what had made that happen. I wasn't sure I wanted to find out. But maybe, someday, I would.

Nobody said much more. It seemed as if everything important had been said. After a while, we walked back to the cabin, Amy singing softly on Grandpa's shoulders. We had some getting ready to do; my parents and Joe were arriving the next day to spend a week at the cabin. I couldn't wait to see them, to show my mother my pictures, to tell my father about the summer. I was even looking forward to seeing Joe, I realized. He would like my drawings, and I had a feeling he was going to like Madame Merlina and Miss Abby, too. And, although I was surprised to realize it, I had missed him.

As we came back into the yard, Aunt Kate put her arm around me, and we climbed the porch steps together. I felt almost weightless, so light and happy and hopeful that only the loving weight of Aunt Kate's arm around me seemed to keep me from floating away.

Grandpa set Amy down so that she could run up the steps ahead of him. Then, as he climbed onto the porch behind her, he suddenly slapped his hand down on the railing and said, "That's it! Knew I'd forgotten something!"

I jumped at the slapping sound, but Amy giggled and slapped her small hand on the railing, too.

"Keep thinking of it when I'm home in the city and forgetting it when I'm up here," said Grandpa. "We haven't done our measuring yet. Haven't marked ourselves on the wall this year. Can't really call it a summer till we've done that, now can we? Think I've grown again, too— none of my pants fit."

"That's not growing, Grandpa, that's too much blueberry pie," I teased as we followed him through the cabin and into my small bedroom, where all our names were mixed up together on the measuring wall.

"Nope, I'm growing, I tell you. I get bigger and better every year. Never did stop growing, and I never will. Make sure you don't, either, Alice Anne," said Grandpa.

"I won't, I won't." I backed up against the wall so that he could measure me.

Grandpa held a book above my head while Aunt Kate drew the line. I stepped away and looked. I wasn't as short as I used to be; I'd grown, already, since the beginning of the summer. The new line was a little higher than the one I'd drawn that first morning. "Alexis Deveraux," it said. It was a little embarrassing, now, to see the name I'd invented for myself. I ought to erase that, I thought. But maybe I wouldn't. Maybe I'd just keep it there for remembering, the way I was keeping the Ouija board.

I took the pencil out of Aunt Kate's hand and wrote my name on the new line, pressing hard to make sure it would show.

"Alice Anne Dodd," I wrote, as plainly as I could, and stood back to study the effect.

My name looked wonderful.